In Love with a Stranger

DIARY OF A MARRIED WOMAN

DR. LINQ Presents

In

Love

With A

Stranger

Diary of a Married Woman

Manuel Johnson

IN LOVE WITH A STRANGER

Copyright © 2015 by Manuel V. Johnson

Published in the United States
Manuel V. Johnson

ISBN-10: 0986143014
ISBN-13:-978-0-9861430-1-4

Talk to Dr. Linq at:
http://www.AskDrLinq.com
http://www.Instagram.com/Ask_Dr_Linq
For input and info, visit:
http://www.Instagram.com/in.love.with.a.stranger

Printed in the United States of America

Purpose

There are millions of women across the world that are just looking for someone that can relate to their troubling story; stories of infidelity, lies and mysterious behavior from their significant other. I believe women from all walks of life can relate to something in this story. I also believe that men who are in relationships can get an inside view on what their woman may be going through just by reading it. In addition, this book has an interesting connection to, "The Mind of a Jerk." I think any reader of that book will enjoy the information they find in this book.

Thank you so much for reading!

In Love with a Stranger

DIARY OF A MARRIED WOMAN

Introduction

His knee planted in the snow, his arm extended towards me. A diamond ring shined from the little black box he was holding. An enormous smile radiated from my face - almost becoming one with the glowing Christmas lights in the park. I said, "Yes," as any woman would; the diamond was gorgeous. Our love has been growing for many years now and this was just the icing on the cake. This much needed trip out of town turned out to be a dream come true. Since a little girl with pink barrettes, playing with my pretend kitchen stove, I always wanted to be a wife and start a family. So that's exactly what we did. We had two beautiful daughters; Skylar, who is now three years old and Brooke - now five. I know he loves the kids and me unconditionally, but after awhile he began to drink and act unlike his normal self. Even the sex became unpleasant. Don't get me wrong, I love some rough sex, but this was different. The vibe I got from him wasn't passion, it was more frustration and his silence on the matter was anything but golden.

***

One evening after a long night of work at the office, he stumbled into the house, his tie untied and draped around his neck. The look on his face was one I had never seen before. He sat next to me on the couch, his elbows on his knees and his eyes gazing into his interlocked fingers.

I asked him what was wrong, he replied, "She's dead."

I jumped up and asked, "Who's dead??!" He looked up at me and said, "It's my fault, I let her die. I knew something wasn't right and I continued with the procedure anyway," he explained.

Being that he's a doctor, he should be use to things like this; this time it was different though. I grabbed his hand and held it tight. I began rubbing his back; he seemed very depressed. I started to wonder why he was so stressed about this particular woman. I understand that a death is tragic, but my husband's reaction to the situation was almost as if I had died.

I asked, "Did you know her?"

He looked up at me and said, "No, I didn't know her at all. But her boyfriend was there and he--"
He stopped mid-sentence and turned his head towards the counter where we had our alcohol bottles. He got up and was about to make himself a drink. At this point, I was starting to get upset with his slow responses. Maybe it was just me wondering about my husband and this woman that has him all shook up.

As he reaches for the bottle I yell, "Mr. Antonio Kinsey, are you going to finish answering my question? *And he,* what?" I asked.
He grabbed the bottle and filled his cup up.

4

He then said, "It's Dr. and No I'm not going to answer your question right now Krissy. I'm really not in the mood to talk about this anymore. I'm home, I'm fine, and the kids are okay."

He took a swallow of his liquor and paused.

He looked around and said, "Where are the kids?"

I smiled and said, "Well tonight…I was thinking…maybe we can have a little time alone. We've been through so much lately. My emotions have been running wild and I know you've been working hard, so I sent the kids to your Uncles house today," I said, while grabbing both sides of his tie, which was still draped around his neck.

He put his cup down and walked off.

Disappointed with his reaction I pleaded, "Aww c'mon Toni. It's been forever since we…you know."

He headed up the stairs and said, "Come to bed, Krissy."

I yelled out, "For what?! You won't even f**king touch me!"

He stopped in his tracks, turned around, and asked, "What did you say?"

Oddly enough, I was nervous, mad, and turned on by the anger I saw in his eyes.

I replied, "You heard me."

He stepped back down the few stairs he had traveled, walked directly up to me and grabbed me by the neck. He then held my head up with one hand. As I was about to open my mouth again, he slapped me in the face! That's when he pulled my face closer to him. We started intensely kissing and lip biting.

He pulled off the flimsy dress I was wearing. Our hands began to explore each other, right there at the bottom of the staircase. In only my panties, he turned me around and made me lean against the wall next to the bookshelf. I heard his belt rattle and his pants drop to the floor. I felt his heavy hands travel across my body, making an indentation at every turn. *SLAP!* He slapped my bottom and I jumped a bit. He pulled my panties down, almost ripping them off and then…he put all of him inside of me. Oh my God, I don't think I can ever get use to his size. After many years of marriage, you would think I am by now.

As he continued to thrust and pull my hair, the books from the shelf fell to the ground. Making a mess, I thought, "Well there's more clean-up work for me." However, that was just a brief thought while we changed positions. He began to go faster and harder and then pleasure turned into just pain. Then he removed himself *from me* and released himself *on me*. He stumbled back and wiped the sweat from his face with his sleeve.

Halfway out of breath he said, "You happy now, Krissy."

I pulled my panties up as he stomped his way up the stairs. I went to the downstairs restroom to clean up. I looked at myself in the mirror and said, *Oh Kristina, Kristina; what are you doing? When are you going to tell him?*

I wash my hands and proceed to the other room where we made our mess. I started to pick the fallen books off the tile. Ah, my favorite read, *"Last Words to a Dying Heart"* by Dr. Linq.

I didn't orgasm that night; but he got his. As long as he's happy, I can live with that; that's how I use to think. He had his way with me at the bottom of the staircase. Well…. when didn't he have his way? It wasn't always like this though. I use to have my way sometimes too. I remember there was a time when he held me different, he

6

didn't touch me with anger or frustration; but rather love. I mean, now his touch feels good, but it doesn't feel like love. Nevertheless, he is my husband and truly I do love him. It's definitely not worth giving up on this family for. Plus he is a doctor and I love to shop. See, we're a team! However, I must admit, things were different before we said our vowels. **Lesson Number 1:** *"When taking a big step forward in a relationship, the next stage may be a bit harder and much more sensitive."* Things changed once we got married, they changed again when the kids were born. They even changed when we moved in this house. Sometimes I wish...let me not say that. But now that I think back, I really started to notice a change in him close to a year ago....

***

Chapter I

SIGNS OF THE TIMES

I wake up to an empty bed, "Toni!" I screamed out. "Where is that damn man?" I whispered to myself. "Antonio!" He didn't respond.

I get up to wash my face and brush my teeth. As I'm brushing, I hear the front door close.

With my mouth full of toothpaste I yell, "Bae, Is that you?"

He replied, "Yeah, I went to the corner store for some gas and a couple lotto tickets."

I rinsed my mouth, walked downstairs and I asked, "Who the hell leaves home and goes to the gas station just to get gas and then comes right back home?"

"I said I played the lottery, I got the gas while I was there baby, calm down," he said.

He always had a way of making me feel like I was crazy. I think men have figured out how to make us feel like we're *always* overreacting. They do a damn good job of it most of the time. But I'm not crazy, I'm in love. At least that's how I see it.

He asked, "What are you cooking tonight babe?"

"I'll figure something out," I replied.

"Well can you make some spaghetti; let's eat *Italiano* tonight," he said.

I laughed and said, "Fool you wouldn't know Italian food if you were in Italy."

He laughed and turned around towards the television.

The girls had been at Toni's uncle's house since yesterday. I grabbed my phone to call them, just to check in - it rung three times and stopped.

Then I heard, "Hello?"

"Hello, Uncle Ray? This is Kristina, are the girls okay?"

"Oh hey Katrina, yes they're just fine. They're in the other room with your Aunt Linda," he said.

I hate it when he gets my name wrong. Nevertheless, he gets it right 50% of the time, so I don't correct him anymore.

I replied, "Ok, well I don't want to bother them. Just kiss them for me, Uncle Ray."

"Alright suga, I will," he said.

Then he asked, "By the way, how's that nephew of mine doing? Tell him I seen him in y'alls new lil blue BMW."

I looked at the phone confused and said, "Umm… Uncle Ray, we don't own a blue BMW."

At that moment, Toni turned around and looked at me as if I called his name.

Uncle Ray then said, "Oh….well you know I'm getting old, suga. Uncle Ray can't see like he use to now; he was kind of far away. Anyway, tell Antonio that I

10

love'em and he needs to come by to pay us a visit. His mother always tried to tell him about how important family is, but that boy never listens."

One side of me was listening to Uncle Ray and the other side was thinking about this damn BMW.

"Ok Uncle Ray, I'll let him know and thanks again for keeping the kids."

"No problem suga, bye-bye now."

I hung up the phone; my eyes landed on Toni who was sitting on the couch. I guess he felt my eyes beaming through the back of his neck.

He turned around and said, "What, why are you looking like that?"

I said, "So we're buying BMW's now?"

"What in the world are you talking about now?" He asked.

"Don't say *"now"* as if I'm always starting something. Your uncle brought this to me!"

I folded my arms and said, "*Now*, Uncle Ray seems to think that he saw you out in *our* blue BMW."

"You want an explanation for that Kris? **Uncle Ray is old!** Did this alleged Toni impersonator speak back to Uncle Ray?"

"He didn't say," I replied.

Toni turned back around and continued watching television. I stood there, even though it all just didn't feel right, I had no proof. **Lesson Number 2:** "*Never bring a knife to a gun fight.*" In other words, until I can come with hard evidence, I'll sit back and build my case. If not, I may find myself stuck with a claim I can't prove.

Later that day, after we ate our *Italian food* and sipped on some punch that Toni made. We cuddled in bed with our stomachs full. The dark room was lit from the glow of the

TV. He wanted to watch the game, but I talked him out of it. I snuggled up under him, inching myself as close as I could get - just being my normal annoying self. I rested my head on his chest as he rubbed on my booty; he knows that puts me to sleep. My eyes began to tighten and my breathing slowed. Then Toni's text message notification sounded off. But he didn't move.

I asked, "You're not going to check your phone?"

"Why? Whoever that is and whatever they want can wait, I'm with my wife," he said.

I assume he figured that would make me feel special or something, *uh...no*. Again, I'm not going to stress the issue. I just find it weird that he's getting a text at 9pm at night. Then again, he has friends and the game is on; it could be anyone.

Five minutes passed and he reached over to grab his phone. Lord knows I wanted to look, but I didn't move. He looks at it for a few seconds and then puts it down. At this point, my sleepiness has worn off. A few more minutes pass and I hear his phone again. This time it only vibrated. He must have turned his sound off. I lie there acting as though I'm into the program on TV. For as long as we've been together, I can't remember a time when he needed to have his phone on vibrate. He's been consistent so far, I hope this isn't the start of something new. My eyes felt heavy and I relaxed...

I open my eyes to a pitch-black room. The clock on the nightstand flashed 12:47am.

"Toni," I whispered. "Antonio!" I said with a little more emphasis but he didn't respond.

I rubbed my hands across the bed to feel for his body, but he was not there. I reached over to the

12

nightstand to lighten up the room, but it didn't come on. The power must be out I thought.

"Toni?" I said a little louder; I'm now starting to get worried.

I then grabbed my phone and noticed the time was 3:17am. I turned my phone around and used the face of it for light. Then I remembered I had downloaded a digital flashlight app. I turned it on and walked towards the window. I noticed the entire neighborhood was without power. As I looked downstairs out the window, I noticed a group of people having a discussion in the middle of the street. Then I see Toni stand out away from the crowd. I then put on some clothes and grabbed my robe.

I turned my light towards the hallway and headed for the stairs. I reach the bottom of the stairway, unlock the front door and walked outside to where everyone was gathered. I see our neighbors, Paul and Stacey Gilmore, a married couple in their late 30s – who as of late have been going through some daunting issues concerning their relationship. Mike and Michelle Worthy; they were another married couple in their mid 50s – a very sweet and helpful pair of souls. Then as an outcast to the group standing alone is Nina Stone. I wonder where her husband Darin is at. Come to think of it, he's probably out of town. A man that's as absent from home as he is has to be causing some friction within their relationship. But that's none of my business; just something that Stacey mentioned.

I walk up to Toni and said, "Hey honey, what's going on; why is all the power out?"

He put his arm around me and said, "We're not sure, baby. I heard a loud crash and then all the lights went out. I jumped up and went to check the breaker box first, and then I came outside to see if anyone else knew what was going on; we were just out here conversing."

Then Nina said, "Seems like we lost track of why we were out here with all of this talking going on." She gave a little giggle and Paul cleared his throat.

Michelle said, "Yes darling, we heard a noise as well. We assumed that maybe a vehicle had crashed into one of the light pole fixtures around here. However, I am not about to walk and find out. It'll be on the news in the morning, darling."

Paul sarcastically asked, "Were you scared in there by yourself, Kristina?"

I replied, "Actually, yes I was, Paul. I woke up in the middle of the night to a dark room and my husband was missing."

"Welcome to my world of waking up every night," Nina said.
Unfortunate for her, I thought; the group got quiet.

"Whelp, I guess we better head back inside and probably burn some candles," Toni said.
As everyone parted ways and said their *goodbyes,*

Nina said to Toni, "Don't forget about me Mr. Boss Man."

He replied very nonchalantly, "I'll put it in for you. A *GOOD WORD*, I'll put in a *good word* for you!" He cleared his throat and turned towards me. Nina was just standing there with this ugly smile on her face. I looked up at him as if I had just caught him cheating or something.

I said, "Uh, excuse me--"

Before I could finish he said, "Let's go inside, honey."

I walked in the house; behind me, Toni closed the door quickly and locked it back.

I turned around and asked, "What the f**k was that about?"

He said, "Listen, Nina's looking for something new in her life. She's going through a lot with Darin being gone all the time - she wants a new start. She's quitting her job for a better position at Mercy Medical - under my direction."

"Hahaha, oh really?" I asked him with a *yeah-right* expression on my face.

"That b***h wants a *new start*, huh? Does the b***h want a new husband too?

Toni replied, "You're crazy Krissy, you know that?"

"And you married this *craziness*. Now give me a kiss and be quiet," I said.

Out of nowhere, the lights turned back on - almost like a sign telling us to cease conversation. I looked out the peephole and the streets were lit back up. Toni turned away from me and began walking upstairs.

"I'm going back to bed," he said.
I turned from the door and headed up behind him.
We reset our clocks and got into bed. I cuddled back under him; laying my head on his arm. The street light shined into the room and I noticed a little twinkle on his chest. I brush whatever it was away and closed my eyes.

7 Am - I'm up and ready for my Saturday morning jog. There's a park with a beautiful jogging trail near the house that I often go to. I like it because it's not too crowded and it's an area where I can be in silence - and I love nature. The Gilmore's were the ones who

showed me where it was. Ever since Paul cheated on Stacey with her sister, they haven't been the same. They use to travel these trails together, now they jog apart. What if, *"A couple that jogs together stays together"* was a true saying? Now that'll be funny. I really need a workout partner to keep me focused; Toni doesn't have the time. Ugh, the story of my life.

I make it to the trail and I began stretching my legs on a tree log at the paths edge. I then hear the sound of tires grinding against the gravel in the park area. The driver quickly parks their car in the closest parking space available. I stop and stare for a second, wondering who could be in this new car. Then I realize I'm being nosey and turn my head back around to finish my stretches. The car door opens and closes.

I hear, "Krissy, is that you?"
I turn around and it's Nina.

I replied, "Mrs. Stone, I didn't expect to see you here this early. I thought maybe you were a *late night* type of runner."

She then said, "I come here to jog regularly. I'm normally here earlier, around 5am, but I had a rough night last night; especially after the power outage issue early this morning. So I figured I'd join the folks who enjoy sleeping in a little longer."
She smiled as she began to stretch with me. I gave her a generic smile back and stood up straight.

"Well I think my body is loose enough now; I'm about to get started on my route," I said.

Nina replied, "Well how about I join you?"
So much for my silence, I thought.

"Sure," I replied.

I look over at Nina dressed in her pink Posh workout clothes with her matching pink waist trainer. I could stand to lose a few waist inches myself; I'm sure Toni would be pleased with that.

We began our slow jog down the parks path.

Nina looked over at me and said, "So Krissy, how do you deal with Antonio's crazy work schedule. I mean, Darin is gone days at a time and when he is in town, he's working 16hr shifts."

I replied, "Well Nina, we communicate and have understanding. I signed up for this. I knew it would be a struggle at times, but you have to do what's best for the progression of the family. Plus, I trust him and vice versa. Hell, I don't even have a lock on my phone. You can't live with something to hide either."

She smiled and quoted what I said, *"Progression of the family"*

She then said, "I like that. One day I'll have a family just like yours."

"One day you will," I said

She continued, "But I would have to imagine that some of those long nights can be lonely in that big house alone."

"Yes, it can be lonely at times I suppose, but--"

Before I could finish she cut me off and said, "You don't ever get…you know…..*horny* alone in bed?"

I slowed my jogging pace down, looked over at Nina and said, "No, Antonio satisfies me enough to last a few weeks."

I was exaggerating, but I just didn't want her to think my husband was neglecting me. **Lesson Number 3:** *"Keep*

your personal problems, <u>personal</u>. It's not always necessary to share.
We slowed down even more and came to a fast walk.

"Look Krissy, I'm sorry if I'm intruding with my questions--"

I cut her off and said, "No, I'll let you know when and if you start *intruding*.
We started to walk slower.

Nina then said, "Ok, well I just wanted to get some advice. I haven't any friends, Krissy. Now it feels like I'm losing my best friend - my husband. I think Darin is having an affair."
We stop completely.

"Aww Nina, do you really think Darin would cheat on you?" I asked.

She said, "I don't know what that man would do."

Then a smile came upon her face and she said, "But that's ok, I met a guy the other day at a corner store on the other side of town. His name is Marcus and girl...he was FINE!"

I stand there shocked that she was open enough to share this with me. Nina and I have never been close. Maybe this was her way of starting a friendship. Maybe I've been looking at Nina in the wrong light. She could just be a lost soul looking for love. But now she's already putting me in the middle of this mess.

I asked her, "So did you two exchange numbers?"

"Yes, he gave me his number on the back of a business card. Krissy, I literally felt him undress me with his eyes. I hadn't felt that wanted in years."
Even though I knew what she was telling me was wrong, I was intrigued.

I asked, "But you're not going to call him or even text him for that matter...right Nina?"

She smiled and paused for a second. I smiled back and my eyes widened with curiosity…"Nina!"

She looked to her left and then to her right; she leaned forward and whispered softly, "I already have."

Chapter II

A CHANGE OF HEART

Cheating; how does someone come to a point where they feel that it's necessary? I always believed that if you have to cheat on someone, you should just leave that person; wouldn't you agree? I guess it's not always that easy though. Someone like Nina has been through a lot it seems, her husband being distant and all. That's still not an excuse to talk to other men. Maybe she always wanted to talk to other men anyway, and now that she has what she considers a legitimate reason - she's using it. On the other hand, maybe she just needs another guy to tell her she's beautiful again. I process all this while we draw closer to the end of the trail.

After Nina told me she had already spoken to the other guy, my response was basically, *be careful.* I'm not good at telling people what they should do with their lives, only when they ask me.

"So do you think I should talk to him?" Nina asked.

Well isn't that just great - she asked me. We get to the end of our trail and begin walking back to the parking area.

Not really in the business of advice, but a tiny bit curious about this new guy, I say, "Ok Mrs. Stone, what's this guy's name again?"

She smiles and says, "Ok, so his name is Marcus." Seeing her excitement I quickly say, "One, why are you smiling so hard? And two, does he know you're married?"

She toned down her smile and said, "Yes, he knows I'm married. I told him I was married the day I met him."

Lesson Number 4: *"If a man still tries to talk to you even when you tell him you're involved with someone else, he probably has one thing on his mind."* Why, because it's clear that you're already taken. However, there are a few things he can still *take from* you while you're married.

I replied, "Nothing wrong with having a few conversations with your male friend, as long as the extent of the friendship stays there."

"Yes girl, it's not going any further. I may never even see him," she said.

We get to the parking area and I wave goodbye to Nina. I didn't drive so I began to walk back home. The trail is right up the street from our house, I figure I can add to my workout if I don't drive.

As I head out on my way, Nina asked, "Hey Krissy, you want a ride? Kind of weird that we're going the same way and one is driving while the other walks, right?"

Yeah I guess she had a point, I might as well hop in with her.

"Ok, sure," I replied.

I get in and notice the new car smell. I look around and notice this is a brand new BMW. Darin must be doing something right on those trips.

I asked, "So when'd you guys get this?"

"Oh, you mean the car? We got it about a week ago," she said.

We make it to my house and she pulled into the driveway. I stepped out the car and closed the door.

She rolled the passenger window down and said, "I had a great time today. We should schedule this more often."

"That'll be great," I said.

"Well take down my cell number," she insisted.

I pulled my phone out and locked in the number she gave me. As she was about to pull off, I looked in the back seat and I saw a brochure for Mercy Medical - the local hospital that Toni works at. Nina really seems like a nice person. Maybe I'll talk to Toni and put in a good word for her. Come to think of it, that probably wouldn't be necessary; he seems to be convinced that she's perfect for the job anyway.

I make it inside the house and the phone is ringing. I left the keys in the door and ran to see who it was – they called *private*.

I answered, "Hello?"

The voice on the other end sounded like a young woman.

"Umm yes, is Tonio there?" She said.

"No, *Tonio* is not here. Who am I speaking with?" I asked.

I was a little upset at the simple fact that this woman was calling for my man. On top of that, she's using her own nickname to address him? I'm the only woman giving out nicknames around here.

She replied, "Well tell him Jasmine called; I need my medicine."

"Excuse me--" Before I could finish my sentence she hangs up the phone.

I set the phone down on the kitchen counter and paused for a minute. So many thoughts rushed in and out of my mind; questions that I needed answered. It's funny how a 30 second phone call can change the perspective of your relationship. **Lesson Number 5**: *"You'll know how fragile your trust is by how easy it's rattled."* I wanted to call Toni while he was at work, but I already know the conversation would end with, *'I can't talk about this right now, Krissy.'* That would just leave me with more questions than I had before. Then I think of Lesson number 2 and I calm down. I'll find out who this woman was in due time. But I know myself; it's going to be on my mind until then.

Later that night, Toni pulls his black Corvette into the driveway. His headlights flash through the living room blinds and across my face. Through the curtains, I see him approaching the door. He opens it and I'm sitting at the edge of the couch with my legs crossed and holding a glass of wine.

"Welcome home," I said.

He asked, "Why is it so dark in here and why are you just sitting there?"

"Don't I brighten up your night enough, honey?" I asked.

I felt his eyes glancing over me as he began to back up and turn around.

"O....K, I'm going upstairs babe. What'd you cook?" He asked.

"There's some *Italiano* food leftover. I've already made you a plate, it's in the fridge," I said.

He snickered and went upstairs. I stayed downstairs and finished my glass of wine. Lord knows I wanted to say something but then I remembered, **Lesson Number 6:** *"Never startle the prey until you're in position to catch it."* In other words, if I mention it now and he is in fact seeing this Jasmine girl, he may start to cover his tracks better - then it would really be hard to catch him. So I'll let the inmates run the asylum...for now.

***

A couple weeks pass; Nina and I have become pretty good friends. We've been jogging regularly, which is great. I guess I found my workout partner after all. She finally got the job with Toni at Mercy Medical. From what she tells me, she's fitting in just fine. I hope that it all works out for her this time. It seems as though me and her have a few things in common now - trust issues. We've been sharing thoughts with each other ever since the random phone call I received about Toni.

My text notification sounds off and it's Nina. She tells me about a big party that's being held at some club on the 1st of next month. Not really my cup of tea, but I think a change of pace may be a good thing.

I reply, "Yes, I'd love to go."

"Ok, great. Trust me, it's going to be fun," she said.

Right as I sit my phone down, the door flies open, "My babies!" I yelled.

Brooke and Skylar burst in and jump into my arms. Toni follows behind them and leans against the door.

"Uncle Ray said they've already bathed, they just need to eat dinner," Toni said.

"We drove in daddy's car mommy - it's fast," Brooke said.

Brooke started floating her hand through the air showing me how her daddy's car was moving. This prompted Skylar to try to crash Brooke's invisible car with her own invisible car.

"Move, Sky! Mommy, Skylar's trying to knock over my car!" Brooke explained.

"Alright you two, since you've been cleaned up, it's time to eat." I informed them while rubbing my tummy – Skylar mocks me.

Toni smirks and walks in the room. He goes to the restroom and turns on the shower. I get up and walk the girls to the kitchen so they can sit at the table to eat.

"Stop!" Skylar cried out.

"Brooke Kinsey, leave your little sister alone, thank you."

"You're always crying for mommy," Brooke said.

I make their plates and I began to make Toni's as well. I still hear the shower water running, so I leave out the kitchen and head to our bedroom. I walk in and I see him in the shower just standing there. I don't say anything, I just watch. It was almost as if he was letting the water wash away his guilt. Maybe I was just looking too far into a blank situation; maybe looking for things that weren't really there. I think of our talks about having a little boy. We've tried to get pregnant again but no matter how many times we've tried, something in me isn't working. I know inside he blames me, but he will never say it. So much so that it seems to not bother him. Now, he doesn't act like he wants a little boy anymore – I guess he gave up.

He cuts the shower off and I walk out the room back towards the kitchen.

A few minutes go by and Toni finally makes his way to the dinner table.

"What took you so long daddy? We're almost done with our food," Brooke said.

"I'm full," Skylar said - her mouth crammed with mashed potatoes.

"Sky, didn't mommy tell you not to talk with your mouth full?" I asked.

She put her head down and started chewing faster. Out of no where we all pause - it's Toni's work pager.

"Damn it," he said.

He looks up at me and I nod my head as if to say, *I know you have to go*. He kisses the girls on top of their heads then walks back to the bedroom to get dressed. The girls finish their food and I take them to the restroom to brush their teeth before I put them to bed.

As I lay them down, Toni kisses me on the cheek and walks out the door. I go to the kid's window to watch him leave. This is getting old; another night will be spent sleeping alone. He's been having a great deal of emergency returns lately. There is only so much loneliness one woman can take. I can see why some women turn to social media outlets for connection. I understand the why, but it doesn't make his absence any easier.

As he drives off, I see a set of headlights approach the back of his Corvette. The car drives past our house and I notice that it's Nina in her new car. I'll admit, for a second I was thinking the worse, but they do work together, so it makes sense....right? All types of images began to flood my mind and the more I thought about it, the more my stomach began to tighten. I flirted with the idea of going to his job just to see if he was actually there. Hmm, I could call Stacey over from next door to come watch the kids while I snoop around a bit. It wouldn't take me but 30 minutes. I pause for a second and began to tap my thigh; something I do when I'm in serious thought. I grab my phone to call Stacey.

"Hey Stacey, how are you this evening?"

"I'm well Krissy, what's going on?"

I replied, "I need a quick favor from you. Can you come over here and watch the girls for me while I head out somewhere?"

She asked, "Okay, for how long? Is something wrong?"

I sigh and said, "That's what I'm going to find out."

She replied, "Say no more, I'll be there in two minutes."

We hung up and I went to go put on some shoes. I grabbed my keys and went into the girl's room. I kissed them both on their heads and waited for a knock at the door.

Knock, Knock. It must be Stacey. I open the door and it's.....Darin?

With a deep voice he said, "Hi, I'm sorry to bother you Kristina. Umm, this may seem awkward but I'm looking for my wife, Nina. She told me you two had been hanging out with each other quite often as of late. I just made it back into town and I wanted to surprise her. When I got home, she was nowhere to be found and her phone was off."

He stood there in my doorway with his shirt halfway open - showing his chest. I'm not saying I was looking or anything…I'm just saying.

His eyes were full of concern. I understood exactly what he felt. Before I could get my first word out, Stacey comes walking across the grass.

"I didn't mean to interrupt the conversation. Good evening, Darin," Stacey said.

"Good evening Stacey," he replied.
She walked pass Darin into the house and went back to the kids' room.

"Well…I believe Nina went to work, Darin. I seen her leave around the same time Antonio left--"
Before I could finish I seen Darin's eyebrows rise with even more curiosity.

I continued, "--*left* to go to work. He had received a page from the office. I'm sure Nina had to go help - she is an assistant after all."

I really wanted to get his opinion on all of this as well, but I couldn't ask a question like that.

He then said, "So I'm assuming that when Antonio received this page, he called Nina to meet him up there. Does that sound about right, Kristina?"
I didn't really think about it that way. I guess he would have had to inform her somehow, she isn't a doctor. That just makes everything more suspicious.

I responded, "That sounds about right, Darin."

He slowly nodded his head up and down and said, "Okay, thanks for your time; Goodnight Kristina. Tell Stacey I said goodnight as well"

"Ok, I will. Thanks and goodnight," I said.

He walked off and I closed the door - well that was awkward. I went back to the kid's room where I find Stacey sitting on the edge of the bed.

She smiled and said, "Look, I don't mind watching the girls, but not if you're using me to cheat with Darin."

"Oh my God! No, Stacey," I replied.
We both laughed. I told her to text me if the girls wake up before I make it back. She said okay and I headed for the door.

I get in the car and make my way to Mercy Medical. I pull up to a seemingly empty building; very few lights were on. I see Toni's car out front and I let out a sigh of relief. At least I know he's at work. I look around for Nina's car but it's not in the parking lot. All of a sudden, another car pulls up on side of me and slowly rolls their window down.

"Darin? Why are you here?" I asked.

"Why do you think, Kristina?" He responded.

"I mean, I know why, but...never mind," I said.

He looked over at Antonio's car parked in its reserved spot and said, "Looks like you found what you were looking for?"
Almost ashamed of finding my spouse while he still hadn't known the whereabouts of his.

I said, "Yeah, it seems so. Are you at least getting a ring when you call her phone now?"

He simply said, "No."

30

"I'm sure she's fine. She might even be home by now," I said.

I was trying my best to keep the situation hopeful.

I then hear what sounded like a phone ringing from inside his car.

He then said, "Well I'm going to drive around a bit longer to a few nearby spots and see what I can find; you be safe out here."

I replied, "Okay you too; tell her to text me when you see her."

He nodded yes and we parted ways.

I take 15 minutes to stop by the store before I make my way back home. I grabbed a scratch off lottery ticket and headed out on my way. I turn on some jazz music and let my window down to feel the breeze of this beautiful night. In route, I pass by a hotel and I see what I believe is Darin's car. I passed by slow then made a U-turn to get another look. Yep, it's him and he's standing next to some key twirling, sneaker wearing girl! I can't believe this guy, his wife goes missing for a few minutes and he's already meeting some other woman?

Wait a minute; I turn the music off and began to think about it all. He was never in town to surprise Nina. He probably lied to Nina about how long he would be out of town on business, all so he could come back in town and cheat with someone who already lives here. It's basically his way of having a free night out the house! He almost had me fooled. I really thought he was concerned about her whereabouts because he felt he was being done wrong. All the while, he's the one doing the wrong.

Lesson Number 7: *"It only takes a few minutes of your absence for your man to cheat on you."*

I snap a couple pictures with my phone and head back home to my kids. Before I went inside I sent Nina a text message, but she didn't respond. I sure hope she has a good story to tell me.

Chapter III

IN THE MIDDLE OF NOWHERE GOOD

I am awakened by the sound of keys flopping against the dresser - it was Toni. I looked over at the clock on the nightstand and it read 6:03am.

"You're just now getting home?" I asked.

"Well good morning to you too, and yes I'm just now making it in," he said.

He then asked, "How were the kids last night?"

"The kids were fine; what was going on at work?" I asked.

He paused, "Umm, well we had an emergency operation; a bunch of confusing medical mumbo-jumbo," he said.

His calm demeanor somewhat relaxed me, outside of the fact that I had just awakened. He stood in front of the closet and got undressed. I played sleep and watched him with one eye halfway open. He walked naked into the restroom and turned on the shower.

He laughed a bit then said, "You know your friend Nina came in too; you should have seen how nervous she was."

My eyes fully opened and I sat up in the bed.

Over the loud sound of the shower water I asked, "So Nina was there?"

He replied, "Yeah, it was her first time being in such a dire situation; but she did well."

I thought to myself, what in the world is going on? I drove by that hospital and Nina was not there; Darin can even validate that. Did someone borrow her car or is he lying? Or maybe she had stepped out for a second. I'm not sure but something is odd. I'll wait to hear from Nina in a few hours, she's probably still asleep.

About four hours later, I get a text message from Nina.

It simply said, "So there's this guy....lol"

I replied, "Nina, where are you?"

"Meet me at the trail in 10 minutes," she said.

I texted back, "Ok."

I get up and get dressed. Toni was still sleep in bed, so I thought.

"Where are you going, babe?" He asked.

I responded, "To the store; you want something?"

He yawned then stretched his arms and legs.

Peeking out from under the cover, he said,

"Yeah, bring me back a lotto scratch off."

"Ok, I'll be right back," I said.

I got in my Lexus and hurried over to the trail - I pulled in and saw Nina's car sitting there. I park next to her and she gets out the car. I too get out and notice the nervous smile on her face.

"Nina, why are we here and where have you been? Darin has been looking for you."

I didn't really give her much time to respond.

"Wait, Darin was looking for me?" She asked.

"Yes, he was looking for you last night? I replied.

"Darin is supposed to be back in town around 12 this afternoon. So what Darin are you speaking of, Kristina?"

She crossed her arms and cocked her head to the side awaiting my response. I had nothing to hide; this was between them two.

I said, "Look, last night Darin came over to my house--"

"He came where??" She interjected.

"Let me finish Nina...He came to our door and he said he was back in town early - he wanted to surprise you. He asked if I knew your whereabouts and obviously, I didn't. Then I saw--"

I pause for a second, because now I was getting to the part where I had to tell her I seen Darin at a hotel with some other girl. But will she believe me? Why would I be out the house at night with my kids at home on a rarely traveled road passing by a hotel? Plus I didn't want her to think I was insecure concerning her and Antonio, even though she has never had any problem sharing her insecurities with me; I'm just not that open.

She asked, "*Then I saw*.....what, Krissy?"

"Oh um, Then I saw that your phone was off when I tried to call you."

She replied, "So Darin is here...in town...now? Do you know where, because he's not home?"

"So you've been home?" I asked.

"Yes, briefly," she replied.

She then said, "Besides, I just passed by our house and the newspaper was still in the yard. If Darin had been home, he would have already picked up the paper. So I'm pretty confident that he's not home yet."

"He was in his car, Nina. So I would assume he probably went inside," I said.

She looked at the ground for a second and then started running to her car.

"Follow me," she said.

"Where are we going?" I asked.

"To my house," she replied with much enthusiasm.

We drive up the road to Nina's house. I follow her inside this beautiful home with marble floors and a small waterfall at the end of the entryway. She looks around for a second then she runs upstairs.

"Wait right here," she urged.

She ran upstairs; I slowly followed up behind her. I watched her enter a bedroom. When I made it to the room, I saw her walk to the front of her dresser where she bent down to pick up a piece of paper off the floor. She hurried and put the paper in a black book that was sitting nearby; I pull my head back out the doorway so I'm not seen.

Then she yelled, "Krissy! Come up here."

I wait a few seconds and entered the room. Nina goes in the restroom with book in hand. I walk over to her dresser and look around a bit. I see a bunch of papers and books by authors I never heard of.

"Come in here," Nina said.

"What is it?" I asked.

Slapping her hand with the book she was holding, she said, "That son of a b***h. He's been here; he left the toilet seat up."

I added, "I figured he was here. Like I said, I saw him in his car last night."

She walked out the restroom before me. I looked around and I noticed she had a bottle of glitter open on the counter; I closed it, turned around and followed her out the bedroom.

As we walked down the stairs I asked, "So where could he be now?"

"Who knows, he's probably somewhere with Jasmine," she said.

"Jasmine?! Who is she??" I asked, remembering the Jasmine who called my house looking for Toni.

She said, "Oh that's just a name I use when I accuse him of cheating. This girl jasmine came to Mercy Medical to visit one of my coworkers named Angie. I heard this Jasmine girl was flirting with Darin one day; it was a day that he came to see me, but I wasn't there. I was out...somewhere, I can't remember. But anyway, ever since then every girl is *Jasmine*."

I asked, "So you're saying she's been to Mercy Medical?"

She replied, "That's exactly what I just explained."

Again I asked, "So Antonio knows of this Jasmine?"

"Umm, maybe so, I'm not sure; something wrong, Krissy?" She asked.

"Nina, a girl named Jasmine called my house a couple weeks back!" I explained.

"*What?* Is it the same Jasmine? What did she say?"

I explained to her how the conversation went between me and this Jasmine girl. I also told her how Jasmine even had her own nickname for Antonio.

Nina asked, "Krissy, why didn't you tell me?" Before I was able to respond, we were both startled by the sound of keys against the door lock. Even though we hadn't done anything wrong, it almost felt as though we were caught.

Nina whispers to me, "Just act normal."

As if I would have acted any other way. Darin opens the door and to his surprise, we're standing right in the entranceway.

"Hey baby!" He said with a smile on his face. He looks over at me and says, "Hello Kristina."

I wave hello as Nina jumps in his arms for a big hug. It was almost as if everything we were just talking about never happened.

Nina asked, "How was your trip, honey?"

"It went well, very well," he nonchalantly said.

Then he asked, "So what were you girls up to?" Nina looked over at me as if I had an answer memorized and waiting on the tip of my tongue.

I said, "Oh, uh, I was here--"

"--to get this book I'm holding," Nina finished my sentence for me.

"Yes, I came for this book here. I've been dying to read it," I said with a nervous giggle.

Nina handed me the book she was holding and I walked towards the door. We said our goodbyes and I got back in my car to head home; I sure hope everything goes alright in there.

Then I started to think about Darin and his whereabouts last night. He made it to the house around 12pm; hotel checkout is normally at 11pm. He set his timing up perfectly. But then that brought me to a bigger question, where in the hell was Nina last night; she never did tell me.

I made it back home and Toni is standing in the kitchen, "You didn't hear your phone ringing? He asked. I reached in my pocket to grab my phone, but it wasn't there.

"Where is my phone?' I asked aloud.

"Don't tell me you lost it again, Krissy. Am I going to have to have them attach it to you by string?" He sarcastically asked.

"No, I think I can manage," I replied.

"Where were you and where are my lotto tickets?" He asked.

Oh my God, I forgot his scratch offs. So focused on their marriage, I'm forgetting about my own.

I sat the book Nina had given me on the counter and walked back outside to find my phone. While in the car looking for my phone, I decided to go to the corner store for Toni's scratch off tickets.

I looked between the seats and found my phone; it was dead. I plugged it into the car charger as I made it to the store. I run in and run back out with tickets in hand. I turn my phone back on and I'm bombarded with text messages from Nina:

- "Hey, I didn't mean to give you that book!"
- "Can you bring it back, ASAP?"
- "Never mind, I'll be over there to get it!"

I make it back home and I walk over to the kitchen counter where I placed the book. I realized it had been moved from where I originally put it; Toni must have looked inside. I wonder why Nina was in such a rush to get the book back. Then I remember she had put that piece of paper inside of it earlier. I open the book to look at the piece of paper and I can't find it - it's gone.

"Antonio!" I yelled.

I wonder if he took it out. As I'm walking to the back to see where he was at, I hear the doorbell ring - it's Nina. Already knowing what she's here for, I hand her the book; she says thank you and runs off.

I go to the back of the house looking for Antonio and to my surprise he's out back on the porch. I walk outside to ask him about the book. Before I could say anything, a cloud of smoke leaves his mouth.

He says, "You know I haven't smoked one of these things in a long time."

He was holding a cigar in his hand. He hadn't smoked a cigar since we'd been married; something wasn't right.

"Toni! What are you doing? I thought you quit."

"I thought I did too," he said.

His calm demeanor somehow made me uneasy, so much so that I almost forgot why I was looking for him in the first place. Oh yeah, the paper in the book.

"Toni, did you see a--"

I'm interrupted by my phone's ringer; it's Nina. I go back inside the house to take the call in private.

I answered, "Hello."

She asked, "Hey Krissy, you didn't happen to see a small piece of paper inside my book did you?"

"No I didn't," I replied.

She said, "Ok" and quickly hung up the phone. I then sat on the couch; looking at Antonio through the sliding glass door. What in the hell has him so stressed out? **Lesson Number 8**: *"Pay attention to the little changes. They may be warning shots for a larger change ahead."*

40

I never asked Toni about the piece of paper in Nina's book, but after a couple days passed, I did ask Nina if she found it. She told me she did, but didn't say where. I guess it's possible that it could have just fallen out of the book during our investigation of her house. Before I was able to ask her about its contents, she changed the subject. I didn't bother bringing it up again. I figured if it was something for me to know, I will eventually know in due time. The truth always shows its beautiful face, even in the ugliest of times. But I'm sure it's nothing that serious.

***

Chapter IV

A FRIEND FROM A FAR

The 1st of the month has arrived and tonight is the night for this big party Nina wanted me to attend with her – it's her day off. Tonight is adult's night so the kids are at Uncle Ray's house. I love them to death but they ran me crazy all week; I can't wait until school starts back. Toni is at work as usual, and I'm standing in the mirror trying on clothes. I have almost every piece of clothing I own on my bed and every shoe out the closet.

Nina texted my phone and asked if I was just about ready; I told her to give me an hour.

She texted me back, "Ok."

Time passes and I figure out what I'm going to wear. I take a few selfies in the mirror and sent one of my pictures to Toni; maybe that'll make his night at work go a little better. I have to show him how beautiful I can be sometimes - can't let him forget.

He texted me back, "Wow, looking good baby. Let me know when you two make it there safe."

"Ok bae," I replied.

With shoes in hand, I go to the counter where my pre-party drink is sitting. I took a small sip and sat on the barstool. I hear Nina pull into the driveway, she gets out the car and I open the door before she rings the bell.

With a smile on her face, she said, "You look nice, girl!"

"Thank you! You do too b***h!" I said as we both laughed at me acting ratchet.

Nina asked, "So you're driving?"

"Nope, not a chance, I've already been drinking," I replied.
Even though I was very capable of driving, it was her party, so her gas.

We make it to our destination and Nina parks her car valet. I text Toni to let him know we made it safe. We get out and I'm already feeling out of place. It's not really my kind of environment, but then I think, what is my environment? Home alone - cleaning? We get to the door and show our ID. I can hear the DJ over the microphone as he transitions from one song to the next. We pay the $15 and go inside.

Nina looks over at me and asked, "Are you alright?"

"Yeah, I'm fine," I replied.

"Yes you are," she said.
I awkwardly laugh and fix my dress, setting my eyes on the bar in front of us.

Nina leans over and says, "We need some drinks."
We walk over to the bar and I began to look around; all while staring at no one in particular. I didn't want to make any eye contact with any guy; he may think it's open season over here. Nina then hands me a drink.

I ask, "What is this?"

"Vodka," she screams over the music.
We walk around for a few and finally rest in one little section for a while. After mingling and enjoying the music for an hour or so, out of nowhere Nina jumps from excitement!

She taps my arm, puts her cup down and said, "Oh my God Krissy, it's Marcus, the guy I told you about!"
Looking surprised myself, I try to see which direction she's pointing in.

I ask, "Him over there in the red and white shirt?"

"Yes," she said.
Well she didn't lie; he was a nice looking guy. His friend looked good as well.

"What's his friend's name?" I asked.

"I believe that's his best friend Mike," she said.
Then with a smile she asked, "You want to meet him?"

"No! I was just curious," I replied.

Nina sat her drink down and said, "I'll be right back." She walked over to Marcus and right as she got close to him, some girl jumped in front of her. I put my drink down, anticipating some sort of conflict. I see Marcus with this stunned look on his face as Nina turned around and headed back towards me.

She grabbed her cup, took a drink and said, "Let's go."
We hadn't been here for more than two hours; I finish my drink and follow behind her anyway.

As we head to the valet, Nina says, "That was Jasmine."

I stopped walking and asked, "I thought you gave that name to the girls you accuse *Darin* of cheating with."

She stops then turns back to me and says, "No Krissy, that is actually Jasmine!"

"Wait, that's the girl Jasmine?" I asked.

She starts back walking, "Yes, that's her."
I can hear the frustration in her voice.

We make it to the car and as we pull off, I saw Jasmine walk outside twirling her keys in her hand. Then a feeling of deja vu came over me; then I realize... Jasmine was the same girl I seen at the hotel with Darin the night Nina went missing! Speaking of her being missing in action, she still hadn't told me where she was that night. Now wasn't the time to ask though.

After a silent car ride home, we arrive at my house. I notice Toni's car in the driveway; I didn't know he was coming home early. I get out of Nina's car and she speeds off. How is she going to be mad and she's the one that's married? Oh well. I ring the doorbell, but he doesn't open the door. I reach inside my purse and fumble around a bit to find my keys. I find them, unlock the door and pushed it open. I walk inside and I see Toni headed towards me.

I asked, "Why are you so sweaty and what are you doing home from work?"
I notice what seems to be a cut on the right side of his chin.

"Is that blood?" I asked.
As usual, I didn't give him much time to answer the questions.

He replied, "I was about to shave when I got home, but when I cut myself I stopped and just came downstairs; it must still be bleeding. I was just doing a few push-ups - that is why I'm sweating. I'm home because I had a slow night at work and I'm home because I pay the mortgage here, any more questions?"

"Yeah, I have one more question," I said.

Who's the owner of the lipstick that's on your shirt?" I asked.
He looked down at his shirt, shocked and caught off guard. As he looked for the lipstick smudge, he kept asking, "Where?" He paused and began to laugh; his eyes rolled up at me and saw that I was smiling.

"Ok, you got me, you got me," he said.

"You were looking like it was a possibility," I replied.

"Not a chance in the world," he said.
He put his arm around my neck and guided me upstairs with him.

He asked, "So how was the party?"

I said, "Ugh, don't even ask! First off--"
I'm interrupted by a sound coming from the downstairs restroom, right next to the staircase we were standing on. Toni kept moving as if he didn't hear the noise.

I asked, "You didn't just hear that?"

"You must have had too much to drink," he said.

"I didn't have too much of nothing," I replied
I removed his arm from around my neck and went back down the few steps I had traveled; I headed straight for the restroom.

"KRISTINA, what are you doing?!" Toni yelled as he hurried back down the stairs.

I make it to the restroom door and open it, turn on the light and I see nothing.

Toni stands behind me and says, "Come on Kris, you're being paranoid."
I turn the light off and began to turn back around.

47

Maybe I am acting a little crazy I thought. Then my woman's intuition tells me to check the restroom closet. I turn the light back on and I open the closet door. Oh my God; my heart drops.

"STACEY?!" I yelled. I had the most confused look on my face.

Right as I was about to grab her by her hair, she looked at me and said, "Kristina, I know how this may look suspicious and...and just all bad. But--"

Toni cut her words short and said, "Listen, let's just get this in the open now. It's well known that I am an attractive man and ever since Paul cheated on Stacey with her sister Lauren, Stacey here has been out for revenge on Paul.

"WHAT?!" Stacey said, as she was surprised by Toni's words.

He continued, "She charmed her way inside; once she got inside, she tried to come on to me. I fought her off and that's how the scratch on my chin came about. Once we realized you were here, we both panicked because we knew it just wouldn't look right. So I told her to hide in the closet. Because even though what she did was wrong, I didn't want you to hurt her, honey. But since you've found out anyway, it's only right that we tell the truth. Baby, I apologize for trying to hide the truth of what happened tonight - I'm sorry."

I take in everything he said; I look over at Stacey just standing there with a perplexed look.

She said, "Krissy.....you can't belie--he's lying, Kris! I swear he literally just made all that up!"

Toni then said, "Come on baby, look at her, she's drunk."

I asked, "Have you been drinking, Stacey?"

48

"Yes," she said.

Toni scoffed.

She finished, "Yes, I've been drinking, BUT HE GAVE ME THE DRINK!"

Her eyes began to swell with tears as she continued on to say, "Look Krissy, I know you love this man and he's your *"everything"*, but he's a manipulative liar.

Now crying she said, "I was up late; just sitting on the porch outside, when he invited me over to have a drink with the both of you, Krissy! I thought you were home; your car is still in the driveway...He came on to me!"

In a disdainful tone, Toni said, "Oh spare us the tears, Stacey. Baby I think it's about time she left our house."

I was so damn confused; I had no words. I went from wanting to drag Stacey out of the restroom closet, to wanting to hit Toni in the head with a bottle of liquor, to just wanting to be alone. Stacey made her way out the restroom and to the front door.

With tears in her eyes, she turned around and said, "Please Kris, he's lying. You have to--"

Toni reached over my head, closed the door and said, "That's enough of that."

"I can't believe you had to find out about her this way," he humbly said as he turned me around and hugged me tight.

In his arms I felt comfort, at the same time I had an unsettling feeling in my stomach.

I asked, "So how long has she been trying to come on to you? And why didn't you mention this to me before?"

He replied, "Because I would have never acted on it. So I didn't see the need to stir the pot. Plus I knew she was going through a lot; I figured she was just a little lonely and stressed. I honestly didn't think her flirting was *that* serious until tonight."

He stepped back and with a concerned look he asked, "You believe me….right?"

I looked back in his eyes, paused for a few seconds and said, "Yes, I believe you."

He said, "Well okay, I think I need a drink."
I walked into the kitchen behind him; I looked back at the front door, thinking about what Stacey had said. He reached in the cabinet to get us both a glass. I saw an empty cup on the counter.

I asked, "Whose cup is this?"

He grabbed it and said, "Oh...I already had one out."

"So, you were drinking?" I asked.

"Uh yes, I had a drink when I got home. Busy night at work," he said.

"I thought you said work was slow tonight and that was the reason for you came home so early?" I asked him calmly, just to show I wasn't trying to start an argument, but was merely curious as to which one it was. He filled his cup up, threw it back and wiped his mouth with the back of his hand.

He put his head down, looking inside of his now empty cup and with just his eyes he looked up at me and asked, "So you think I'm lying, Kris?"
Never had I seen that look in his eyes before. I didn't know a simple question warranted such a gaze. His hands began to shake as though the anger inside of him was building and waiting to explode.

I replied, "Well, I wouldn't say you're lying--"
As I began to speak he slowly made his way around the kitchen bar and closer to me.

A bit nervous I continued, "I umm…..I was just curious, concerning which one it was; were you busy or slow?"
He smiled, which made me feel a little at ease. Then at that very moment he grabbed me by my neck and with one hand he lifted me off the bar stool on which I was seated. He held me up as I scratched at his hand, hoping he'd let me go; my feet dangled just inches from the ground.

He screamed, "**DON'T YOU KNOW I LOVE YOU, KRIS?!**"
Unable to respond I tried kicking him. That was when he finally let me go and I dropped to the floor gasping for air. Out of breath and afraid, I remained on the kitchen tile as he walked past me. I then heard his keys rattle and the front door opened and rapidly closed. As I lay on my back staring at the ceiling, I see his headlights flash through the curtains as his car pulled off. I cried silently as if I was holding it in on purpose. But then I couldn't control it and it just overwhelmed me. In a matter of seconds, I had a face full of tears and a pair of blood red eyes.

Oddly enough, the tears didn't last long. It was like an emotional switch clicked off and my crying stopped. I wiped my face and got off the ground. I grabbed the bottle of liquor that was still on the bar, walked over to the couch and took a seat by the window. As I glanced outside, I swallowed what was left in the bottle. **Lesson Number 9**: *"Sometimes love hugs you tight and tells you everything will be okay. But sometimes love grabs you by the neck and drops you on a kitchen floor. But what's important is* *how you respond to it after it's done what it's done to you."* Or maybe love has nothing to do with this situation at all.

Chapter V

OLD TO ME - NEW TO YOU

Days of near complete silence turn into weeks of little words. Ever since that night Toni and Stacey were in this house alone, Toni and I haven't been speaking much. It's almost as if we've become strangers in this house. He apologized and I've accepted his apology. Besides, his apology eventually led to this new pink diamond ring. I personally don't think that situation is worth giving up on my marriage for. I mean, I didn't *see* anything happening between them. Name one couple that doesn't fight sometimes. He had a drink or two and plus I questioned his love for me; so disrespectful of me. At least I know he truly loves me, right?

I haven't seen Stacey around lately. It's almost as if she's been avoiding me whenever I come outside. She'd normally stand in the yard and care for her plants around sunset. Now it seems as though she waits until it's dark out. I don't know, but if she *was* telling the truth, I'm the one who should be embarrassed to come outside, not her.

Even though Toni and I haven't been the best of friends as of late, he has a birthday coming up in two weeks. Before this incident, I had plans on giving him a surprise birthday party. I've debated with myself on whether or not I should still have it. I asked Nina for her opinion, she said I should go ahead and do it; she probably just wanted the free drinks. But after some thought, I finally decided that I'm going to go along as planned. I'll tell all the guests to bring gifts, that way I won't have to get anything big for him! I just have to figure out who I'm inviting.

I go to his desk where he keeps his tablet, just so I can get in contact with some of his friends and acquaintances. I find his tablet under a stack of books and papers. Luckily I've seen him unlock it before, the code is, "**7, 1, 4, 4**." I click on his *Contacts* folder and I begin writing down names and numbers. I don't want it to be too big of a party so I write down just a few names; mainly the ones that I've heard him mention from work. Coworkers, a few family members and our neighbors, that should be more than enough.

As I was about to lock his tablet back, I saw his *Gallery* folder just sitting there. I wonder what pictures he has in here. I click on it and the first image I see is Toni naked in the mirror of our bathroom. What in the hell is he taking pictures like this for?? Especially if they're not being sent to me! I continue to swipe; I didn't find anything else odd. But I did however find some random pictures of the kids, his car, and me, but that was about it. As I'm about to get up from his desk, I look and see a piece of paper with the words, *"Call C. Thursday."* I move the papers in front of me so I could glance at the desk calendar; today is Wednesday. Who is this C. he's calling Thursday? The b***h receiving his d**k pictures?!

I paused for a second and calmed my *overreacting* a** down. I'm sure the two have nothing to do with one another. When I'm home and he's not around, my mind is everywhere. Ever since the Stacey incident, I've just been a little...I guess *paranoid* is the word. **Lesson Number 10**: *"It may take a decade to build it with blocks of love, but it only takes one dance with the tornado of doubt to blow it away."* Once the trust is rattled, it takes awhile for it to stop shaking and get back to its calm and steady state of being.

The evening comes and Toni finally makes it home. The kids have already eaten and are just about ready for bed. Without them, I don't know where I'd be. If no one else loves me, I know my kids do.

I prepare Toni's meal while he's in the shower - the usual routine. He comes in the kitchen to get his plate. He stands behind me, kisses me on the cheek then takes his plate into the TV room to eat.
I go to the kids' room to make sure they're tucked in. Once I get them in bed, I go back into the TV room to sit with him.

Five minutes of complete silence and then while still facing the television, he asked, "So what'd your friends say about your new ring?"
I looked down at my finger; I'd forgotten I had it on.

I replied, "What friends?"

He snickered a bit and said, "What friends, huh?"

"Yes, you know I don't have many friends," I said.

He turned his head from the TV and with a serious look on his face he asked, "So your ex boyfriend or none of your new little boyfriends said they liked it?"

"Wait, what??" I asked, while displaying the most confused face of all time.

"My ex boyfriend?? I haven't heard from him in years! Why would you even mention him?"

Toni replied, "You seem to be getting very defensive right now from such a simple question."

"A simple <u>minded</u> question - a <u>stupid</u> question," I said.

He put his fork down, wiped his mouth with his napkin, and went to put his plate in the dishwasher. I remained seated on the sofa, thinking he was returning to the TV room.

He looked over at me from the kitchen and asked, "Can't take a joke?"

He then walked off and went to the bedroom. I sat there on the couch, wondering what in the world would make him say, "*Ex boyfriend.*" The way he asked, as if I'm the one with something to hide. Knowing damn well that I don't have any wants or reasons to speak with my ex anymore.

A joke... really? That must be his way of using sarcasm; I didn't find it funny at all. But then I thought about **Lesson Number 11:** "*Guilty cheaters love company. Even if they have to build a situation that was never there.*" If he thinks that he's going to paint me as the bad one by bringing up random guys of my past, all while he's actually cheating, he has another thing coming.

The next day comes and I'm going over my list of names and numbers for the party invites - calling and leaving voicemails. I get halfway done with the list and notice the name *Calvin* with a phone number next to it. I laugh because my ex boyfriends name is actually Calvin. See, this goes to show that my ex wasn't even on my mind. I wrote it down yesterday and didn't think about the name once. Only reason I'm thinking of my ex and this name of his, is because Toni indirectly mentioned him. I sit there, staring at the name and number; tapping my pen against the kitchen table. I grabbed my phone and called it - it rung twice.

A man answered, "Hello?"
The voice on the other end was a voice I knew all too well; I immediately hung up. I sat there for a minute and thought to myself, what in the entire hell is going on?! That was definitely my ex Calvin, but why does Toni have his number? Then all of a sudden, my phone rings and it's Calvin's number. In a matter of seconds, I debate whether I should answer. But then I figured, I'm a happily married woman, well maybe not *that* happy as of late, but you understand what I'm saying. I'm secure, kind of…..Oh God, just answer the damn phone Kristina.

"Yes?" I answer with my innocent voice.

He replied, "Hi, I'm sorry, did someone just call me from this number?"
I then went on this long spill, trying my best to explain why I was calling.

"Umm…yes, yes, well…Hi, I'm Mrs. Kinsey, Antonio Kinsey's wife. I was throwing him a surprise birthday party two weeks from now, on Thursday. I wanted to reach out to all of his friends, family and associates, just to invite you all to this event. *But* see here's the thing, I just realized that I might have over invited. Yeah, it seems like it probably won't be enough room for everyone, so mid-call I hung up. I'm sorry about that sir, but you have a wonderful day."

I tried to hurry and hang up the phone, but he stopped me before I could and with a comforting voice he said, "Nice to speak to you Mrs. Kinsey and thank you for the invite. I guess it wasn't meant for me to be there, because next Thursday I'll be busy. I'm scheduled to clean an office space right outside the city. That's what I do ma'am, I clean buildings. In fact, I'm glad I'm able to speak with you. Your husband and I spoke about me cleaning the floors at your house I believe. He saw how my team and I did at the hospital, so he wanted to hire me for personal use, he said. You wouldn't happen to have any knowledge on the matter would you?"

I laughed on the inside and thought to myself, see this is why me and him never worked out, he couldn't even recognize my voice.

I replied, "I'm not too sure, sir. I believe he already hired someone else for the job, I'm sorry."
Yes, I was lying, Toni and I hadn't talked about having our floors cleaned, let alone someone he hired. But Calvin didn't know that.
I could hear the disappointment in his reply.

He said, "Well that's too bad…..that's just too bad. Well thank you Mrs. Kinsey, you have a wonderful day ma'am."

I replied, "Ok sir, you too, bye-bye now."
I almost felt bad for him. But there was no way in hell that he's coming to this house. What was Toni thinking?? Toni had to have known who he was; maybe that's why he mentioned "ex boyfriend" yesterday after dinner. But just because *he* has Calvin's contact info, doesn't mean I did too. Hopefully I never hear from him again.

***

Two weeks passed and it's the day of the party. In about five hours, this house will be full of people. Some I like and some I couldn't care any less about. I have everything prepared and ready for Toni when he arrives tonight. I encouraged everyone to be here at 7pm. Toni said he should be home around 8pm. So that should give everyone enough time to get here and get settled in before he walks through the door to receive his "*Surprise*!" I advised everyone park their cars at the trail so Toni wouldn't see them when he came home. I asked our neighbor, Michael, if he would stay at the park so that he could bring everyone here once they've made it there. He agreed, but I believe it's because he wanted to get away from his wife Michelle for a while. Also, to look at the women on the jogging trail; but that's none of my business.

A few hours passed and I'm just about ready; I still got that magic party planning touch. As I put my finishing touches on the event's setup, I hear a knock on the door.

"Who is it?" I asked while I tiptoed up to the peephole.

"It's Stacey!"

I dropped back down, took a deep breath, put on a smile and opened the door.

"Hello, Mrs. Gilmore!" I said with much excitement, trying to lighten the forthcoming tension; it worked.

She replied, "Hey Mrs. Kinsey! How have you been?"

"I've been just fine, Stacey. Thanks for asking.

I asked her, "How about you?"

"Everything is well, everything is going well," she said.

We stood there for a brief second, staring at each other

and smiling. She then looked down at what she was holding.

"Oh! Here's some cheesecake for your party," she said.

"Wonderful, I'll keep this for Toni's personal stash. Cheesecake is his favorite."

"It's mine too," she replied.

She seemed hesitant to come inside the house.

I asked, "You're not staying?"

She replied, "I don't know if I'm comfortable with that, Krissy."

I didn't want to go back and forth with her about it, so I simply said, "Understood."

We said our goodbyes and I closed the door behind her.

7Pm and people are really starting to arrive. Thanks to Michael for being my transporter this evening, Toni won't even know what's going on inside. I greet everyone at the door; I have them sit their gifts in the corner, out of the way of the coming partygoers. The doorbell rings again and I rush over to open it for the next set of guest.

"Hey, Krissy!" It's Nina and Darin.

"Good evening Kristina," Darin said.

"Listen to him, Krissy; *'Good evening Kristina',*" Nina mocked how formal Darin's greeting was. We all laughed and they stepped inside to join the festivities.

"You two can sit your gifts right over there in that corner."

"Okay…Kay," Nina replied.

Darin nodded his head in compliance to my request.

I get everyone's attention in the house and I explain to them that Toni should be home in an hour. I tell them where we're going to set up our *"Surprise"* scare and then I let everyone know that I truly appreciate their presence and presents. I then go upstairs to change clothes.

"Oh, and everyone…please do not, I repeat *do not* touch that cheesecake in the refrigerator! Besides me, that's going to be Toni's personal treat tonight," I said. Everyone laughed; I turned the lights off in the main room and went upstairs. I fixed my makeup, did my hair, and put on my clothes that were laid out on the bed already. So far the night is going well - let's hope it stays that way.

My phone rings and it's Michael.

I asked, "Getting tired yet?"

He replied, "Kristina, I think I just seen Antonio pass by the park. You guys might want to get ready!"

"Oh my God, okay bye! Oh and you can come back now, Michael!"

I looked in the mirror one last time and hurried downstairs.

"Ok everyone! This is not a test; this is the real deal. The birthday boy should be pulling up any second now! Turn off the music and get into your positions."

Everyone huddled in the designated area, awaiting his arrival. Then we see the lights from his car shine inside the house. He comes to the door and rings the doorbell twice. I wait a few seconds, then I open it; I greet him with a hug and kiss.

"Well you look stunning tonight," he said.

"Thank you baby," I replied.

He asked, "Why is it so dark in here?"

He walked towards the TV room then headed for the kitchen.

That's when I hit the lights, "*SURPRISE*!!"
Everyone screamed!
It scared the hell out of Toni; he jumped and dropped his newspaper. We all laughed and he did as well.

"Wow! This is amazing! You all really kept this a secret from me, huh?! See, I can't trust any of you! Everyone laughed even harder and we all gave him our birthday wishes.

"If I would have known this was coming, I would have worn something a little more appropriate for the party," he said.

"Don't worry, we all know the circumstances," Nina replied.

Toni looks over to the couch and said, "Uncle Ray, you made it too? Where's Linda?"

Uncle Ray replied, "She's home with the girls. She said she would have liked to have come, but she just hasn't been in a good mood since the surgery, nephew."

"I understand Uncle Ray," Toni replied.
The music starts back and everyone starts enjoying themselves again. Toni makes his way upstairs to change his clothes; I follow behind him. As I'm heading up, I hear the doorbell ring again.

"Nina, can you get the door for me? It's probably Michael coming back from the park."

"I got it," she replied.
I turn around and follow Toni to the room.

I ask, "So you like the party?"

He said, "Yeah, It's very nice. Thank you, babe."

I stood up from the bed, grabbed his hand and said, "You know, Toni, I feel we--"
knock, knock. Nina was at our open bedroom door.

She said, "Umm, I don't mean to interrupt, but Toni, someone's here to see you."

62

"Tell them I'll be down in a second," he said.
I sat back down on the bed.

Toni put on his shirt, bent down, kissed my forehead and said, "We'll finish this later, okay?"

"Okay," I replied.
I watched as he followed Nina downstairs.

Sitting for a minute or so, I heard loud laughter coming from the TV room. I got up and went downstairs to see what was so funny. I see Toni laughing with some guy who has his back towards me.

As I approach the two of them, Toni looks up at me and says, "I don't believe I've introduced you to my wife yet."
The man turns around and it's my ex boyfriend, Calvin!

Toni continued, "Kristina this is Cal; Cal this is Kristina."
My facial expression was blank. Calvin on the other hand seemed to be in complete shock.

I shook Calvin's hand and said to Toni, "Can I speak with you in the other room for a second? It'll just take a second."

Toni replied, "Sure honey. We'll be right back Cal."

As we walked off, Calvin said, "Nice meeting you Kristina."

"Yeah," I replied.

We make our way to the guest room; I grab Toni by the arm and asked, "What the f**k are you doing? Why is *"Cal"* in my house, Antonio?"

"He cleans floors and porches, plus he owns his own cleaning service. And he's damn good at it," he explained.

Getting frustrated; I asked, "Who…invited…that man…into…my house, Toni?"

He replied, "What does it matter, Kris? Look, here's what's going to happen; you're going to go back out there and enjoy the rest of the night. You have nothing to hide, right?"

I look into Toni's eyes, confused as to why he can't just find another floor cleaner. But fine, I have nothing to hide.

"Right," I replied.

Toni smiled and said, "*Good*."

We walked back out to the party where everyone was at, as if nothing happened.

Toni walked back up to Calvin.

He then said to Toni, "I can leave if there's a problem."

Toni laughed and replied, "Problem? There's no problem, you're my guest; enjoy the party!"

Toni put his arm around Calvin's neck and walked him to the kitchen where the other guys were. Calvin looked back at me and I turned my head so I wouldn't make eye contact. The front door opens and it's Michael; he finally made it back from the park.

"Hey Kris, did I miss something? Where's Toni?" He asked, so oblivious to the mental strain I was going through.

I pointed towards the kitchen and he went on his way. I seen a drink sitting on the shelf in front of me, I threw it back and sat the glass back down. Let me try to enjoy the rest of this odd night the best way I can.

Chapter VI

IN TIME OF NEED

I t's been a week since the party took place. Our marriage is pretty much at the same standstill it's been at. I want to move past my trust issues, but he doesn't seem to want to make that possible with his recent silent treatment. Lately he's been working really late and that doesn't make it any easier. But no time to dwell on that, I have to remember, **Lesson Number 12:** *"Never stress over the things you can't control."* All I can do is my best; I can't force anything on anyone.

It's still early in the day, so I decide to head over to the park for a quick jog. Toni was still in bed as I got ready; he was going to work late today I assumed. As I finish getting dressed, I get a text message from Nina.

"I really need someone to talk to right now," she said.

"Ok, I'm headed over to the park for a little morning exercise," I replied.

I asked, "Want to meet me there?"
"Ok," she said.
Oh lord, I'm sure it has something to do with that Marcus

guy. She seems to stress over him just as much as she does her own husband. But hey, I'm not one to judge.

I get in my car and head over to the trail. As I pull into the parking area, I see Nina sitting on the bench.

I step out my car and asked, "Uhh, where are your workout clothes? I'm not jogging alone, sweetheart."

She looked up at me and said, "Me and Darin are getting a divorce."
I then sat down next to her on the bench.

"What?? Why, Nina??"
She went on to explain, "Last night after a great time spent together, I took a shower. While showering--"

She paused and started to tear up a bit; she took a swallow and continued, "...while showering he sat on the toilet next to me; out of nowhere he just came out and admitted that he had been cheating!"

I was lost for words, but I wasn't surprised. I felt bad that I never told her about the night I saw Darin at the hotel. But I guess the truth will come to the light anyway - one way or another.

"Aww I'm so sorry, Nina."
I was trying my best to comfort her. I put my arms around her as she began to cry on me.

After she composed herself, she kept going, "Krissy, he was cheating with Jasmine!"

I immediately told her, "Look Nina, it's not your fault. He's a selfish pig for that! It has nothing to do with you; *he's* the one with the problem! We as women always are faced with these type of issues. I'm sure with time you two can possibly work it out."

She looked at me, wiped her nose with the napkin she was holding and said, "He also told me he's gay. What does that even mean, Krissy??"

I blurted out, "You mean bi-sexual?"

Her face straightened up and she said, "Gay, bi-sexual, tri-sexual, Triceratops, I don't care, Krissy! He's giving my d**k away!"

Her sadness began to turn into anger and frustration; sprinkled with a hint of confusion.

She said, "I'm taking half of everything, the house, the cars, the accounts; everything!"

I then told her, "Well first, let's see how this all plays out before we start talking about--"

She cut me off and said, "I'm done Kris, I...am...done, girl."

She giggled a little as she said it, but I knew she didn't find any of this funny. But what else can you do but laugh when your heart is bleeding inside?

I asked, "So Darin isn't staying in the house, right?"

"I told him he could stay; I left," she said.

I then asked, "So where are you going to go?"

"I don't know yet, maybe my mother's house."

She then mumbled, "God, I can't believe this is happening."

Being that I already felt bad about not informing her of Darin's *hotel run* before; I figured I could at least make things right by letting her move with us until this little incident got resolved.

I said, "You know Nina, if you want you can stay with us until you and Darin work out the kinks of this situation. I'm sure Toni wouldn't mind."

She looked at me, smiled and said, "Thank you so much, Krissy. Where would I be without you as a friend?" I smiled and gave her a tight hug. We get up from the bench and walk back to our cars.

"So where are you headed now?" I asked.

She put her big black shades on and said, "I have to go meet someone and inform him of some bad news; I'll talk to you later, Kris."

"Okie dokie; Talk to you later," I said.

We pulled out the park - I went one way and Nina the other.

Now back home, I began to look inside the guest room, seeing what I needed to remove or replace for Nina. Even though I feel bad for her, an incy wincy bit of me feels a little better thinking that maybe this Jasmine girl wouldn't have the time to be in Toni's face. I'd rather it be her husband than mine.

I go upstairs to run the idea of Nina staying with us by Toni - he's up and in the shower.

He stepped out the shower and I told him, "Darin and Nina are getting a divorce."

He froze.

"What happened??" He asked.

I explained to him everything that Nina explained to me.

He then said, "Wow. I guess a couple weeks won't hurt. But remember, just a couple weeks; nothing more. This isn't a shelter home; I see Nina enough at work."

"Speaking of work, did she say she was coming in?" He asked.

I said, "You know what, I'm not sure. She said she had to meet some guy."

"Some guy?" He asked.

"Well she referred to the person as '*him*', so I would like to think it was a guy. Why?" I asked.

He replied, "Oh, nothing, nothing. She's scheduled to come in today, that's all."
He finished getting dressed and I undressed. Then I thought…Damn it, I didn't even get a chance to jog this morning.

Toni grabbed his protein shake and breakfast fruit bowl out the refrigerator. He gets in his car and heads off to work. That's funny; this morning was probably the most we've talked in a while.

The kids are asleep and will be up soon. I go in the kitchen to start cooking them some breakfast. Once I finish, I sit down and turn on the TV. All of sudden I hear the doorbell ring. I peak out the window and see a work van sitting in the driveway. Whoever it is, they aren't standing in front of the peephole.

"Who is it?" I asked.

"Dirt Or Nah," the guy on the other side of the door said.
Who in the hell? I open up and Calvin was standing there in my doorway. I thought, what kind of cleaning service name is, "Dirt Or Nah"?

"Calvin, what the hell are you doing here?"

He said, "Well good morning Mrs. Kinsey. I'm scheduled to clean the carpet in your TV room. Your husband said you guys had a couple spills during the party you had a few days back. I'm also here to pressure wash your back patio, ma'am."

I replied, "Look, please stop with the 'ma'am' and 'Mrs. Kinsey' stuff. Come in, do your job and leave, okay?"

"No problem Mrs. Kins......I mean, Kristina", he said smiling as if he knew something I didn't.

"How have you been anyway?" He asked.

"Stop, I said <u>do your job and leave,</u>" refreshing his short term memory.

"Sure thing," he said.

I walked back to the kitchen to grab my phone. I wanted to call Toni to let him know what was going on. I finally got a hold of him and told him that the cleaners were here.

He simply said, "Okay, fine," and rushed me off the phone.

I guess he must be having a busy morning.
The kids wake up and rush downstairs, I send them both right back up to brush their teeth and wash their faces. They run upstairs and I go to the kitchen to make their plates.

I yelled upstairs to the girls, "Hurry up! Uncle Ray will be here to pick you two up in a little bit!"
Summer will be over soon and they'll be back in school. No more playing in Uncle Ray's and Aunt Linda's big backyard playground with the neighbors kids; just school books and cute outfits.

After the girls eat their breakfast and play a bit, Uncle Ray pulls up. I tell the girls to grab their bags from upstairs.

He said, "Well good morning, Katrina."

"It's Kristina. Good morning Uncle Ray," I said, while trying to correct him without making it such a big issue.
Then from behind him I saw Aunt Linda. She hadn't been to our house since the first year we moved in.

I smiled and asked, "How do you two make it work after so long?"

She looked at me and smiled.

She walked closer and while putting her hand on the side of my face, she said, "Love is a wild animal. It can push you to give your all or it can push you to kill all. It's only the cage of trust that keeps it tamed."

Wow, I thought to myself.

"Thanks, Aunt Linda."

"You know I told her that," Uncle Ray said.

"Aunt Linda replied, "Oh hush you old lying dog." Uncle Ray and I laughed.

The girls come running out the door by me.

"You're not going to say bye? Come give mommy a hug," I said.

They turned around to give me some loving.

As they pull off, I wave goodbye. I then look over to my left and saw Calvin, eyes squinted from the sunlight; he was staring right at me; standing at the side of his van, grabbing what looked to be his pressure washing machine. My smile disappeared and I went back inside.

I walk back into the kitchen to wash the dishes. As I'm standing there washing, I look out the window to the patio area. I see Calvin instructing his worker on where to move our chairs and tables for the cleaning. Then Calvin takes his shirt off. I turned my head and looked back down at the dishes. Somehow, my eyes found their way back up to him. By default, thoughts of when he and I shared better times together came into mind. Then thoughts of him walking out on me reminded me why those better times meant nothing.

In the middle of these useless thoughts, I feel two hands grab me by the waist!

"Gotcha!" It was Nina.

"Girl you scared the hell out of me, what are you doing here? How'd you even get in here?" I asked.

She grabbed a hand full of grapes out the fruit bowl on the counter and said, "One, I'm sorry. Two, I live here now. *Bloop!* And three, you must have left the door unlocked."

She looked outside at Calvin, leaned closer to me and continued, "I guess you weren't...*focused* on locking the door."
She popped another grape into her mouth and smiled.

"Get off of me," I said while laughing. "Girl, nobody was looking at them."

"It's okay to look, Krissy. You just can't touch," she said while placing another grape on her tongue.

She went on, "Notice I said YOU can't touch; mmm...I like chocolate!"
Funny how she said, *you just can't touch*. When last I checked, she was about to touch all over her lil friend at the club.

"You mean like how you didn't touch Marcus?" I rhetorically asked.
She threw a grape at me and I ran off laughing.
As if I'd really take advice from her. I'd probably end up in the same place she's in. I'm glad she's in good spirits though; she sure wasn't earlier today.

Chapter VII

CLOSER WITH DISTANCE

We've gotten the guest room cleaned out and Nina has moved in while her and Darin go through all their legal issues. Being that he works for a law firm, I hope she doesn't get the short end of the stick. It's been about four weeks since Darin confessed his cheating to her and for one of those weeks she's been staying with us; so far so good. She normally just stays to herself in her room and I can't blame her. In a time like this, you probably just want to stay secluded from everyone else.

She and Toni are at the hospital today; I kind of feel left out. But I'll be back working soon. I want to start my own business again. I can't imagine working for someone else anymore. Why help someone build his or her dreams when I can build my own? I wanted to try something in the fitness world. But Toni doesn't think it's a good idea for me…And he's a doctor! You'd think he would push me towards that, but nope, not my husband.

Toni and I haven't had sex in weeks. There's three ways I relieve stress: sex, cleaning and shopping. I put on some clothes to go downtown to do a little shopping for the house. I really wanted to get a new patio set for the backyard as well. The old one has faded a bit; time to upgrade.

I text Toni, "I'm going downtown to do some shopping - any request?"

"What store are you going to?" He asked.

"I'm not sure, maybe Furniture City," I said.

He replied, "Oh ok. No request here, do what you do best."

I didn't know if that was a compliment on my decor skills or an insult to what he feels I do all day.

Then I get a text from him saying, "Ask Nina if she needs anything for her room."

I thought, *ask Nina*, for what? What in the hell could she possibly need for a guest room and if she did need anything, she could get it herself. I don't work for her.

I texted back, "Isn't she there with you?"

"No, she had to go to court today," he said.

I had forgotten all about her court date. I thought she was at work; I can't keep up with her schedule. Well I'm not asking her anything anyway. He really pisses me off sometimes.

I change the subject and asked, "When will you be coming home?"

"I'll be home early today," he replied.

"Ok," I said.

I make it downtown to Furniture City and I look around a bit. I talked the store employee down on the price for this beautiful patio set they had only one left in stock too. I can see myself sitting at the table now,

74

reading my favorite book and sipping my diet tea. As I'm having this beautiful thought of tranquility, I'm startled by the clearing of ones throat. I turn around and it's Calvin.

"Hello Kristina."

I immediately begin to speed walk away. He grabbed my arm to stop me.

Then he pulled me close and with a low tone said, "Kay, listen--"

I cut him off and said, "Do not call me Kay."

He went on, "**Kay** listen, I don't want every time we see each other to be a bad moment of bad memories."

I replied back, "One, let my arm go and two, I agree with you. So how about this...how about we don't see each other at all, deal?"

He let my arm go and I walked away.

As I'm leaving, the store employee yelled out, "Mrs. Kinsey, my manager said everything is good on the patio set. Only problem is that for the price you'll be getting it, we cannot deliver it for you. You'll have to find a way to take it home and you'll have to find that way today. We can't hold this deal for you."

Well isn't that great. I didn't have room in my car to take the set home today! I tell the store employee to just cancel the deal. I start on my way back out the door to leave.

"I have my truck outside, I can bring it home for you right now," Calvin said.

I pause for a second, my face scrunched up because I really didn't want to have to use his services, but damn, I really want this patio set today, ugh.

I turned around and said to the store employee, "Sir, I'll take the patio set."

They load it all up on Calvin's truck and he follows me home. He begins to unload the truck and we go to the backyard to set it up. He moves all the old patio furniture and I explain to him where to place the new furniture. There was one large table that needed to be put together.

He looked at me and asked, "Should I get my tools?"

I looked back at him and in an annoyed way I said, "Go ahead."

"He laughed and said, "If you don't want me to put it together, I won't."

"No, no, you can," I said.

"Oh, so I'm not good enough to talk to, but I'm good enough to do free work for you," he replied.

"Shut up before I change my mind," I warned him.

He smiled and went back to the front of the house to get his tools for the table. I stood there and smiled a bit. He came back around the corner and I put my serious face back on.

He then said, "Kay, you remember that time I put that dining room table together? Remember the first night we sat at the table, it collapsed and all the food I cooked was wasted?"

I just stared at him as he kneeled down to start putting the table together.

I replied, "Yeah, I remember. Then I fed the food to the neighbors' dog and that dog crapped in everyone's yard for the next 2 weeks."

He paused and said, "Wait, so you're the reason I had to keep picking that dog s**t out our yard??"

I burst out laughing, nodding my head to say "yes".

He laughed along with me.

"God damn it, Kay! Are you serious?"
I couldn't do anything but laugh. I remember one day
Calvin had fell in the dog poop and cursed the neighbors.
I thought it was funny then and I find it hilarious now;
especially since after all these years he's just now finding
out that it was because of me.

He said, "That's f**ked up, Kay."

I shrugged my shoulders and said, "Hey, one day
I'll buy you a cup of coffee for your troubles."
He smiled; I guess he took that literally.
Our laughter now dies down and an awkward silence fills
the area. I coughed and put my *serious* face back on.

He cleared his throat and said, "So, what are you
going to do with the old one?"

"I'm sorry the old *what*? Oh the furniture! Umm,
well my *husband* talked about giving it to the neighbors to
sell in a yard sale for us."

He stood up and said, "Oh, well I want it. How
much is it worth to him?"
His eyes were piercing through my shirt.

I had a feeling he wasn't talking about the old
furniture anymore.

I approached him and said, "It's worth more than
you make in a year."

I then walked away and said, "Call me when
you're done with the table; and leave your shirt on this
time."
I could feel his eyes watching me as I left.

He then loudly replied, "That means you were
watching!"
I didn't respond, I just kept walking back to the house
with this stupid smile on my face; then I caught myself.
What the hell am I smiling for? I walk to the kitchen
window to see if he's back working. That's when I felt a

hand rub across my back. It scared the, *you know what* out
of me! It was Toni.

"Hey Babe, who's truck is that outside?" He
asked.

"Oh hey, umm.....off early...that's right," I
nervously said.

"No just waiting for a 2 O'clock appointment," he
replied.

He asked again, "Kris, the truck?"

"Oh...the truck! Well see--"
Before I could finish getting the words out, Calvin comes
in yelling for my attention, "Aye Kay!"

"Who the f**k is *Kay*?" Toni asked.

"Oh Mr. Kinsey; didn't know you were here."

"Did it matter, Cal?"

Calvin paused then laughed a little, "Umm, I'm
sorry, I was just here to put together this patio set Mrs.
Kinsey had purchased at the furniture store today."

I interjected, "Yes...yes, oddly enough I ran into
Calvin down at Furniture City and they had this deal that
said I had to take the set home today in order to receive
the discount. Long story short, Calvin loaded it up and
brought it home. He was just finishing with the table that
needed to be put together."
Toni stood there with an expression that spelled anger.

Toni turned towards Calvin and asked, "So is this
table complete?"

Calvin replied, "Umm yes, yes. It's just about
done."

"Ok, so you wanted "*Kay*" for something?" Toni
asked.

Calvin replied, "Oh right."

He then turned to me and said, "Mrs. Kinsey, on
the table you have out there you have the option of

78

having gold or silver leg bottom attachments. I could put on either one."

I told him, "Gold."

Toni jumped in and said, "Silver."

Then he looked down at me and continued, "Because when it rains and the gold gets old, it's going to start to look faded."

He then turned his head to Calvin and said, "... and nobody wants old things."

Calvin cracked a little smile and said, "Ok, Silver it is."

I dropped my head as Calvin made his way back outside to put the finishing touches on the table.

Toni grabbed his newspaper he had sitting on the counter and left out of the kitchen.

A few moments later, I saw Calvin get into his truck and pull off. I was full of all type of mixed emotions. Toni has to remember that Calvin is my ex. I mentioned having an ex boyfriend named Calvin and I even showed Toni a picture of him a year or so ago. Is he trying to use Calvin so he can have a reason to be mad at me? He can't just be around for the floors, or maybe he is.

Later that night I tell Nina about what happened. She seems so fascinated with Calvin, as if she wants to talk to him herself. I don't want him, but being that he's my ex, I don't know how I'd feel about her talking to him. Well I actually do know, *hell no*. If she's my friend, that means he'll be around here even more probably. But after what happened earlier today, he may not be at all.

Nina laughed at me as I explained to her what happened and called me and Calvin's little exchange, "healthy flirting". I personally wouldn't call it that, but whatever. Then I remember part of lesson number 11. Nina was a guilty cheater and it sounds like she's excited at the <u>idea</u> that I may be a potential cheater. But trust me…. I'm far from one.

Just a couple days passed and the girls were back at home. We decided to eat dinner in the backyard on our new furniture. Nina joined us in the breaking in of our patio set. The girls are getting along with her; they call her *Auntie Nina*. It's unfortunate that she hasn't been able to have kids. She probably would have been a very loving mother.

"Kris, can you pour me some more juice?" Toni asked.

"I'll get it, Krissy. I was going inside anyway," Nina said.

"Oh, ok….thanks," I replied.

"Thank you Nina," Toni said.

"No problem boss man," she replied as she got up from the table to refill his glass.

Boss man, huh? I couldn't help but think about the last time I heard her call him that; the night we had that blackout awhile back.

She made it back and handed him his glass; I excused myself from the table at that moment.

I got up and waved the girls on to follow me inside.

"Come on girls, time to go and get ready for bed."

"Aww man," Brooke said.

Sternly I replied, "No whining Brooke. Come on Skylar, you too."

Nina asked, "Need some help?"

"I think I can manage," I said.

"Girls, it's past your bedtime; follow your mother upstairs," Toni added.

80

"Yes sir", said the girls in unison.

As I was bathing the girls, Brooke asked, "How long is Auntie Nina going to stay with us, mommy"

"Not too much longer, baby. Auntie Nina's only here because she had some bad people at her house," I explained.

Splashing in the water Skylar said, "I like Auntie Nina."

I mumbled, "*Don't we all.*"

After the girls washed up and I tucked them in bed, I figured Toni would have found his way into the house by now; I go downstairs to see what's going on. I see Toni and Nina outside laughing on my patio set. I step back into the shadows so they don't see me. I stand there and start to second-guess Nina staying in this house. I haven't seen any foul play, or anything that would make me believe they're doing something behind my back, except the fact that he's a man and she's a woman. But other than that, there's nothing solid. Then they both raised their glasses to have a toast. I come out from hiding, figuring it was about time I broke this little physician fiasco up, Nina gets up from the table to head inside. I play it cool as if I was heading towards the kitchen.

"The girls are asleep?" She asked.

"They should be," I said.

"They're so beautiful. I was just telling Toni how I wish I had girls of my own," she said.

I laughed and with a hint of sarcasm I said, "Well you can't have mine."

She smiled back and said, "It's getting late; dinner was fantastic, Kris. I'm going to bed now."

"Night-Night, Mrs. Stone", I said as I made my way to Toni.

I heard Nina echo from around the corner, "Not for long, baby!"
Her divorce should be over soon. Good, she'll be out of this house without me having to kick her out.

I make my way over to Toni who's still sitting outside, now smoking his cigar - I notice a wine glass in front of him.

I ask, "Is that liquor?"

"As a matter of fact it is. Would you like a taste?" He asked.

"No thank you. You coming to bed now or you're going to drink and smoke a little longer?" I asked.

"Why are you acting so bourgeois? Relax," he said.

"Relax, really? How am I *not* relaxed?" I asked.

He continued, "I'm saying, lighten up a little, that's all. You know what; don't worry about it, Kris."

He took another toke of his cigar and blew the smoke into the air. I inhaled some of it and started to choke a bit. "*Cough, cough*"

"I'm going inside," I said.

"See you in a bit," he replied.

As I turned around and made my way inside the house, I hear a room door close. Nina must have just made her way back from the kitchen or something. She better not be eating in that damn room.

I go upstairs and get into bed; I can't sleep until I know Toni is in bed with me. I then hear the sliding glass door close and seconds later footsteps on the stairs. Toni walks in the room and gets into the shower.

After he finishes, he comes to bed.

His last words were a mumbled "good night" before the snoring began.

I lie there thinking about my life, my relationship and where they're both headed. I'm really not feeling loved; and I don't like it. Maybe Toni's right, maybe I do need to lighten up a bit. Or maybe I just need some sex from my damn husband! That may help too, no?

Chapter VIII

PUSH AWAY

A beautiful Saturday morning and I'm awakened by the sound of birds chirping outside my window. I decide I want to get some sweets from a downtown shop called, "Cakes, Cookies & Coffee". I been there once before and it was great. I figured I could bring some treats home for everyone. I knock on Nina's door to see if she wanted to tag along.

"Nina, you want to ride with me downtown to Cakes, Cookies & Coffee?" I asked.

"No thanks, I have a headache," she said through the door, sounded like she was under the covers still. Alone I go - that's a good thing; I rather be alone anyway. Nothing wrong with wanting to get away from everyone, is it?

I'm headed downtown and I notice a black car making the same turns as I am. Almost as if they're following me. Once I make it to my destination, they drove past - false alarm. I pull into the shops parking area and I notice a familiar truck in the first parking spot. I get out and as I suspected, Calvin is inside. I walked over to where he was.

"Ok, now I think you're following me," I said.

"Kay! Funny meeting you here."

"*Funny* how?" I asked.

He stood up to pull out my chair then sat back down and continued, "I was just thinking about you." I blushed a bit, I'll admit.

I replied, "Really? Thinking about me? Is that all you got?" I asked.

He laughed and said, "No, but I'm glad to know that you're curious about what I have." I cleared my throat and wiped the smile off my face.

"Curious? I'm not curious. You always were a comedian," I said.

He grabbed my hand and said, "Some things never change."

I snatched my hand back and firmly asked, "What in hell do you think you're doing? I am a married woman," I said as I showed my ring.

He replied, "Married to whom? I heard how he talks when you're not around. I saw how you look at him. You don't want to be there."

I replied, "You know what…you have a nice morning, sir."

I got up from the table to leave; he jumped up and began calling my name until we were both outside standing in front of the building.

He said, "Kay, look I'm sorry. I just…..I just feel we never really ended on a good note and when I seen you at that party….I was….you look gorgeous, Kay. Better than I could have ever made you look. You're happy, I understand. You know I've always loved you and always will. But you're married now and I'm trying my best to respect that."

It was the first time in a long time I had someone tell me I was gorgeous. He was right; we never did end on a good note or even with an official separation. It was one of those situations where you just fall apart. Then one night Calvin never came home. I ended up moving out our townhouse and eventually met Antonio.

Calvin walked off and headed back to his truck.

I blurted out, "Hey…. don't I owe you a cup of coffee?"

He looked back at me, looked at his truck and said, "You see how the Law of Attraction works?"

I said, "Oh please, don't start with all that Universe stuff again. You got some explaining to do, sir."

We walked inside and we got everything off our chest. He explained that the reason he left was because he was afraid of failing me. At the time, he'd lost his job and I was the breadwinner of the house; I was a personal party planner at the time. He said he just couldn't accept the idea of being *taken care of* by his woman. It made him feel less of a man. I explained to him that as his woman, that's what I'm supposed to do when my man falls on hard times. Actually, running away from financial stresses makes you even less of a man. It's funny how I went from being the breadwinner in one relationship, to being the bread eater in another. By the time we're done, we were both laughing and giggling like old times.
We walk back outside and said our goodbyes.

He said, "I think I still have your number from when you called me about the party. I'll give you a holler."

"Umm, no, you won't," I said.

"Oh stop it, Kay. Now I owe you some coffee", he replied.

I got in my car went on my way back home. I didn't even realize I was gone for the majority of the morning.

I get home and when I open the door, I notice some of the books from our bookshelf on the floor.

I yell out, "Brooke! Skylar! Which one of you two made a mess down here?"

I sniff the air, something smells funny I thought. I look around to see if I left some dirty laundry out, but I see none.

The girls didn't respond. I notice my favorite book; *"Last Words to a Dying Heart"* fell as well.

"Damn it - Brooke! Skylar!" I called for them again.

Toni came from the bedroom and stood at the top of the staircase, he then said, "The girls aren't in here."

"Well, where are they?" I asked.

Wrapping his robe tighter around his waist he said, "They just woke up not too long ago. They're out back with Nina, playing that Twister game now."

"You just got out the shower?" I asked.

"Yeah, how'd you know?"

"Your hair looked wet," I said.

"Where were you at this morning?" He asked.

"Oh, I was at Cakes, Cookies & Coffee, Nina didn't tell you? I asked her if she wanted to go this morning. She told me she had a headache; glad to see that she's feeling better now."

"Yeah she seems to be doing okay. So did you bring anything back?" He asked.

I was so wrapped up in the conversation with Calvin I forgot to bring something back for everyone. I knew I had nothing on me, but I looked down at my purse as if I had a cake inside of it.

"I didn't think anyone wanted anything. Everyone was sleep anyway," I said.

Toni walked away and went back into our room. I got down on one knee and picked up the books that had fallen. I notice what looked to be drops of water on the wood floor. With just my eyes, I followed the trail of water from the bookshelf and noticed they led to Nina's room. I stood up, then looked upstairs and then looked to the backyard. Nina and the girls where still outside playing. I went upstairs to our bedroom where Toni was. While he was in the restroom shaving, I walk in behind him and through his robe, I start rubbing on him - just to see if it gets hard. He rinsed his face and dried his hands with a near by towel.

"What are you doing?" He asked in a relaxed tone.

"Obviously nothing, you aren't getting turned on," I said.

I stopped what I was doing and backed away.

Toni started laughing and asked, "Why'd you stop?"

I didn't find it funny at all.

I asked, "What's so damn funny?"

Trying to hold his laugh in, he said, "Nothing, Nothing."

I walked out the bathroom

"What's the matter, he's all used up for today?" I asked.

His smile disappeared as he followed behind me.

"What the f**k is that supposed to mean?" He asked.

"You seem to be getting very defensive right now from such a simple question," I sarcastically said.

I walked out the room and headed towards the front door. I see Nina coming inside the house from out back.

"Hey Kris," she said.

I ignored her then went out to my car and just sat there. I grabbed my phone and scrolled through it. Sitting there, I realized that I literally didn't have any friends. My only friends were the ones I now lived with - and that's slowly falling apart.

After dinner that night, Nina pulled me to the side and asked if she could have a word with me.

I asked, "You have something you want to tell me?"

"Yes, I do," she said. I don't know how to tell you this, but I'm a little concerned about Antonio.

"Concerned about *my* Toni; how so?" I asked.

Nina continued, "Well during lunch time the other day, I seen him getting in his car with some woman."

My eyes opened and my heart began to race.

"With who?" I desperately asked.

"I'm not sure," she said. "I hate to say this but it looked an awful lot like Jasmine."

"Oh hell no, she's already messed up one of our marriages. She's not messing up mine!" I firmly stated.

Nina leaned in closer and said, "Look, before you mention this to Toni, let's wait and see what we can find next."

I said, "You're right. Then I hit him with what I found! That way he can't deny it!"

Nina agreed, "Exactly!"

90

"I'll keep my eyes peeled for you," she said.

I gave her a hug and said, "Thanks."

I walked out the room with mixed feelings. If this Jasmine girl is still around, she better not touch my husband. On the other hand, I don't know how I even feel about Nina and Toni's friendship right now. Yes, I know they work together so of course they're going to be friends, but that doesn't mean I have to like it.

As I'm heading upstairs, I hear what sounded like someone falling. Then I hear Skylar begin to cry.
I rush upstairs to see what's going on.

As I head towards her, I cry out, "Sky baby, you okay?"
Toni was holding her trying to calm her down.

I asked, "What happened?"

"She fell trying to stand on that stool." He said. "She probably bruised herself."

"Aww my poor baby; give her here," I said.

"I got her. Let me go into the bathroom to get a better look," he replied.

He took her to the bathroom to look at her leg.

Nina came to the bottom of the stairs asking, "What's wrong with Sky?

I hear Toni say, "Bring daddy's phone, Brooke."
I start walking downstairs, telling Nina about Skylar's little incident.

"Aww not my Sky-Sky," she said.

"She'll be alright," I assured her. "She's a big girl, like her momma."

Nina smiled. I went back upstairs and as I was turning the corner, Toni was opening the bathroom door.

"How does it look?" I asked.

"Not to bad, it'll probably be worse tomorrow," he said.

I reached out to grab Skylar; he then handed her to me. I grabbed a tissue from the box on the hallway table.

"See Sky, you've gotten your *Fuzzy The Bear* shirt all wet with your eye rain. You have to be more careful, baby."

Still sniffing, she nodded yes to signal her understanding. She'll be fine.

***

A few days go by and oddly enough, Calvin and I have been talking regularly. Yeah I know I said I wouldn't. But damn, I can't chat with an old friend? On this particular day, around 3 in the afternoon, the house phone rings.

I answered, "Hello?"

At first the person on the other end said nothing, but as I was about to hang up, a soft voice said, "Is Tonio there?"

"Who is this?" I asked.

"Jas," she said.

"B***h, don't call my mother**king house no more!" I said furiously.

I slammed the phone down and the battery fell out the back. I couldn't believe she had the nerve to call my damn house…again.

"Toni!!" I screamed.

He came from out the kitchen. I run up to him with my hands all in his face.

"Who the f**k is Jasmine?" I asked. "And why in the hell is she calling for you?"

"First of all, calm down," he said.

Nina comes out her room, goes in the kitchen to grab the girls to take them out back.

"I shouldn't have to feel like my husband is hiding something from me," I explained. "This has gone on too damn long. If you have something you should tell me, TELL ME!"

In an untroubled manner he said, "Well for starters, you're acting crazy in front of the kids."

"The kids are outside now, so talk!"

He nonchalantly replied, "I don't know any Jasmine. Maybe she--"

"BULLS**T!" "That's bulls**t Toni and you know it! If you're f**king her, just be a man and tell me!"

I don't know why I was so upset; I lost it. I mean, I know *why*, but this wasn't really my character. But I knew that in my gut he wasn't being truthful.

Lesson Number 13: *"When the love is deep, sometimes it digs treasures inside of you that you never knew were there."* We went back and forth and he continued to deny even knowing a Jasmine, but I knew that was a flat out lie. But without *proof* of them talking, I couldn't *prove* anything.

Chapter IX

TWO WRONGS DON'T

I left the house and just drove; I didn't have a clue where I was heading. I guess the road was kind of like my life; open both ways with no particular way better or worse than the other. Then unexpectedly I got a text from Calvin.

It read, "Kay Okay?"

"No Kay not Okay?" I replied.

He texted back, "I knew I felt something. See how the universe works?"

I sent back, "lol"; but I wasn't laughing at all.

His next text said, "Well if you need someone to talk to, I'm here."

"Where is here?" I asked.

He sent me his address and I put it into my GPS.

A few minutes later, I arrived at a nice townhouse not to far from the downtown plaza. As I'm getting out, I look around, just surveying the area. I saw a black car park about two houses down the street, a neighbor bringing his trash can inside and some kids playing with their racecars.

I ring the doorbell twice and he opens up. He stood there shirtless in a pair of blue jeans. I notice he still had "Kay" tattooed on the right side of his chest; I thought he would have had that covered up by now. I guess the more things change the more they stay the same. I started to feel a little uncomfortable with being there - I am technically married. But at the same time I felt wanted in his presence and that was a good feeling.

He greeted me at the door, "How's it going, Kay?" He asked.

"Everything is going about as good as it has been," I replied.

He started walking down the hallway of his house - I followed behind him.

"Things will get greater later, I'm sure of it," he said.

"Yeah well I'm not so sure," I replied.

"You have something you want to get off your chest?" He asked.

He led me to a couch where we sat in front of a wall mounted TV. His place wasn't big, but definitely something more suitable for a single man. Then I realized that I never asked him if he was actually single.

"So where's Mrs. Calvin Harris?" I asked sneeringly.

"He smiled and said, "Well…she doesn't exist anymore. To be clear, I wasn't married; we were in love though. I feel that's the most important thing and everything else kind of follows behind that."
He stopped himself and put his hand on his head.

"Where are my manners?" He said. "Would you like something to drink? I have alcohol, wine, and malt liquor."

"Really, Calvin?"

We both laughed. He then offered me a glass of water. While he was in the kitchen, I stood up and looked around a bit. I seen old pictures on a shelf he had by the sliding glass door. As I'm looking at his photos, I see a man in his backyard.

"Do people always walk through your yard?" I asked.

He said, "Yeah, it's always some idiot around here, walking somewhere he shouldn't; probably the neighbors."

He brought me the glass of water and then opened his window blinds to see if the guy was still there. He came and sat back down next to me.

"Thank you," I said.

"You're welcome," he replied. "Ok, so where was I?"

"You're still in love with your ex," I jokingly said.

"I wouldn't quite say it like that," he replied.

"But I remember where I left off now, thank you."

I smiled, nodded and toasted my glass to him.

"But yes, she and I separated a couple years back. She eventually found someone else, but we stayed in contact throughout and even talked about getting back together. The next thing I know--"

He paused for a few seconds. Then turned his head and began to tear up. I put my hand on his back and rubbed him for comfort.

"I'm sorry," he said. "...next thing I know, she umm.... she died."

He let out a sigh and continued, "…she died in the hospital; in their care. How that happens to a perfectly healthy woman during a pregnancy is beyond me. Regina…Regina was her name."

"Oh wow, I'm so sorry, Cal."

He wiped his face and said, "Yeah, well don't worry about it; you didn't do it, ya know."

I looked him in his eyes and he glanced into mine. I put my hand on the side of his face and with my thumb, I wiped his last tear away. Our faces floated closer to each other, almost as if we weren't in control of them. My heart began beating faster and my breathing was more noticeable. Then…our lips touched and from there, my body took control of any rational thoughts I may have had. His hand cupped my breasts as our tongues met. I hadn't felt this in so long, and I mean that literally. It had been so many years since Calvin touched me this way. We paused to remove our shirts. Now topless, Calvin just stared at me.

"Wow, you're a work of art. I can'-- I can't do this," he said.

"Stop talking," I told him, as I pulled him on top of me.

I felt like I was 17 again, being a bad girl on someone's couch; but it felt so good inside to feel *wanted* and lusted over.

He turned my body straightforward as he got on his knees in front of me. He reached for my jeans and unbuttoned them. As he pulled my pants down, I rose up a bit so he could slide them off easier. He started kissing from the top of my foot and worked his way up to my inner thigh. His wet tongue traveled down in between my legs and he began kissing me through my panties. I could

98

have climaxed from that alone. I start squirming in my seat as he pulled my panties completely off; I damn near screamed when his tongue touched me! In a matter of seconds, he had the couch wet and me even wetter. I grabbed the top of his head and then the back of his neck as I started to grind against his face. The more I moaned, the more he licked, which in turn made me moan even more. Then he flipped me over, made me put my knees into the couch and pushed my head down so that my a** was in the air. He began kissing and softly biting my a**. He then finished putting his tongue all up and down my kitty cat.

Now he was facing upward, he slid his head between my legs and said, "Sit up straight."
He made me ride his face while he spanked my a** then gripped my hips to assist me in my *ride*.

Then I felt my legs become weak and my pelvic area tightened as I screamed, "I'm cuming!! I'm cuming!!" I tried to get up, but he held me down on top of him. It felt like I was about to die - it was too intense!

"Ok….ok…I can't…." Out of breath, I pleaded.
He was moaning and then started slurping whatever was left dripping out of me.

He got up and said, "Let's get in the bed."
Breathless and numb, I could not move. He picked me up and carried my naked body to his bedroom.

He laid me down and asked, "You ready?"
Even though I was NOT ready, I said, "Yes."
I was still recovering from the first orgasm. He loosened his pants and they dropped to the floor. He was already hard and pointing directly at me. It was like his d**k was pointing me out of a lineup. While still on the bed, I crawled towards him on all fours. I then wet my hand and grabbed his d**k and began stroking it. It's not that it's

only long, but it's so thick too. I could barely fit my fingers around it. I almost forgot how it felt to hold it in my hands. I kept stroking it while he leaned his head back and moaned.

"Do you have a condom?" I asked.

"Of course," he said.

"Ok….just making sure."

He walked over to his dresser and pulled out his gold wrapper. I lie there on the bed touching myself while he put the condom on. Next, he climbed on the bed towards me. He started licking my thighs again, so I pulled him up and we started tongue kissing.

"Oh my god," I said as he was sliding inside me. We started slow, kissing and enjoying each other's body.

He whispered, "I miss you, Kay."

Hardly able to speak, I said, "I miss you too." Then he rose up onto his knees, grabbed my waist, and started to f**k me faster. Occasionally he would drop back down to suck on my breasts. He grabbed my neck, started choking me and proceeded to trust harder.

"You're about to make me cum again, oh my god! You're about to make me cum again!" I screamed while his neck choking muffled my words.

He then asked, "You gonna cum on daddy d**k for me, baby?"

"YES, IM CUMING BABY!" Twice!

He turned me on my stomach, I couldn't take anymore; I just rested there. He f**ked me from behind until I felt him shaking.

"Come on, daddy. Come for momma," I said.

Momma can't take anymore; I thought to myself.

He yelled, "Ahhh, I'm cuming!"

"Yesss, baby!" I yelled back.

He fell on my back for a second, still inside of me. Then he pulled himself out.

"Ahh s**t," he said.

He caught my attention immediately; I asked, "What's wrong??"

"Oh, umm nothing, nothing, I just washed these sheets," he said.

I laughed, "Too late to think about that now."

He joined me in laughter and said, "I know right." He got up and flushed the condom down the drain. He brought me a wet washcloth, but I told him I was going to shower before I left anyway. Then it hit me, damn, Antonio. I remained calm while Calvin began talking; I couldn't hear anything he was saying. My husband, what the hell have I done??

The pleasure was good…okay great, but this isn't me. I guess Calvin could see my mind was somewhere else.

He asked, "Something bothering you?

He pulled me closer to him and I got comfortable on his chest.

"I'm fine…I just….I'm fine," I said. My response probably made it look worse.

"You can tell me anything, Kay."

I took a deep breath and said, "Okay. My husband, I love him. I know after what we just finished doing, that may sound strange; but I do. But as a woman, sometimes I have needs that just can't be pacified with words. The sad part is that I don't even get the words from him."

I sat up in the bed to get more of a face-to-face conversation with Calvin. He remained relaxed against the headboard.

I continued, "He's been very distant and I almost seem to be nonexistent to him; socially and sexually.

Calvin stepped in, "Sexually? How is that even possible with a body like yours?"

"It's not always about looking good, Calvin. Our marriage should be passed that by now," I explained. **Lesson Number 14:** *"Every beautiful creation has someone who takes its beauty for granted and someone else who can't take its eyes off of it."*

I then said, "I've been receiving phone calls from another woman."

"On your cell phone?" He asked.

"No the house phone," I said. "Plus, my best friend is in the middle of a divorce right now; that just makes me more insecure about my own marriage. Now she lives with me and works with Toni. I was worried about their relationship, but she told me she thinks she saw Toni at work with another woman. And I figured she wouldn't tell on him if they were actually seeing each other because….ugh, never mind. I don't know; I'm one big mess."

He asked, "So your friend Nina, who also works with him, saw Toni with another woman?"

I paused, "How did you know her name was Nina?"

I saw his eyes open wider as he sat up in the bed.

"Oh….well she works at the hospital with him. I saw her there a few times; very pretty woman. She's the one who invited me to the birthday party. I thought you knew that.

I jumped up off the bed; completely confused.

"Wait; can repeat what you just said?"

He laughed a bit and said, "I saw her--"

I cut him off, "After that."

He repeated, "She's the one who invited me to the birthday party?"

I smiled and dropped my head, "That's what I thought you said."

Wow! I was lost for words. Why would Nina invite my ex to a birthday party for my now husband? What would she be trying to accomplish? I stop and look out the bedroom door; I see my clothes scattered in Calvin's living room.

He then said, "I have something else to tell you, Kay."

But I didn't have time for any more sentimental talk with him.

"Oh my God, I have to go!" I nervously said.

I ran out the room to get dressed.

"What's wrong?" He asked.

"I shouldn't have come here, I shouldn't have f**king come here," I said, as I slid my panties back on.

He asked, "I wasn't that bad, was I?"

I ignored him and continued to put on my clothes.

"Hey, I thought you were taking a shower," he said.

"I was, but not here, not now," I replied.

"So you gonna just *hit and run*? Who's running away from whom now?"

I finished putting my clothes on; then walked to the door and before I walked out I said, "I'm sorry…and thank you."

"No thank you; you helped me more than you know," he replied.

Before I closed my car door, he said, "Maybe you should see an attorney."

I nodded and said, "Maybe so."

As I'm pulling off, I see a car pull out behind me. What made it so noticeable was the fact that it looked like the same black car I saw following me before. Again, they made sure they kept their distance. This time I made four complete right turns, just to see if they'd follow me, they didn't. Maybe I'm just a little paranoid. *Not being myself* is a wave I seem to be surfing on as of late.

I pull into the driveway and I notice Toni's car isn't home. I unlock the door and I'm greeted with silence. No one seems to be home at all; I immediately head for the bathroom to take a shower. When I'm done, I stand there seemingly still alone in this big house. I walk around just staring at the pictures on the walls and all the things we've bought to fill our home with. Realizing that items aren't what make you happy, happiness comes from within and no one can just hand it to you - only you can hand it to yourself. **Lesson Number 15:** *"You have the key that unlocks your happiness within. Finding that key may be difficult at times, but understand that finding it is necessary in order to have a fulfilled life; a life that is lived in its most beautiful form."*

After a few hours of my alone time, Toni and the kids make it home; I didn't see Nina with them. I didn't ask where she was either and I did not care. Toni and I didn't speak, I didn't feel the need to say anything; I guess the feeling was mutual. I got the kids ready for bed as usual and went out back to sit at the patio. Looking down at the table, I began thinking about what Calvin said about contacting an attorney. Then it hit me, I knew just the perfect person to speak with.

Chapter X

THE ENVELOPE

I'm up bright and early to start my day. Toni was already gone to work. Today I took the girls to Uncle Ray's house. Mommy had some important business to handle. I take the interstate headed to the law office on the other side of town.

I walk inside the building and after a few words with the receptionist I see a very familiar face come from the back.

"Hello Kristina," he said.

"Hi Darin, how have you been?" I asked with a very welcoming smile.

His smile seemed to be of nervousness; I'm sure my presence was alarming.

He replied, "I've been well; just trying to figure everything out."

"So what brings you in the office today?"

I looked around the small office space and asked, "Is there any place we can talk in private?"

He was a bit taken back by the serious look on my face.

"Uhh…yeah, sure. Janine, hold my calls," he said to the receptionist.

"Yes sir, Mr. Stone," she replied.

"Follow me this way, Kristina."

We walk down a long hallway and veered off to an office room in a back corner.

"You like to have your distance from everyone I see."

"Yeah, I like to work in my little corner of the world alone," he said.

He pulled out the chair at his desk for me to have a seat. He loosened his tie a bit and sat down.

He leaned back in his chair and asked, "So, how can I assist the wonderful Kristina Kinsey this beautiful morning?"

I smiled briefly and said, "I think Antonio and I may be moving towards getting a divorce."

He leaned forward and his lazy posture changed and began to match the seriousness of my words.

"I'm so sorry to hear that; I truly am." He then asked, "But why...what happened?"

I took a deep breath and said, "It's nothing official, but I have seen too many little things happen. I feel it in my gut that he's seeing someone else. I've had women call my house and... I don't know anymore."

I can see the concern in his eyes, but he can't relate; he's on the other side of the situation. Maybe he knew what was going on in Toni's mind.

"Kristina, you must understand that divorce is a serious issue - you have a lot to consider. You have kids with Antonio and that can be such a mess if you two end on a bad note. Correct me if I'm wrong, but I believe he generates the majority of the income in the household, so you'd probably receive alimony, but nothing permanent."

I took in everything he was saying and the more I listened to it, the more I wanted nothing to do with it.

106

He continued, "As you know, Nina and I are going through a situation of our own. She came to me and said she wanted out. I told her I'd done nothing wrong and I've only tried to make sure she had the best things in life. She's always--"

"I interrupted, "Wait, you did nothing wrong?"

"Not to be in you two's business but I heard just the opposite," I said.

He sat there with a befuddled look on his face. Clearly he didn't know anything about this alternate story - why is he lying to me?

"What did you hear, Kristina?"

"Well, I was told that you came to Nina one night and admitted to sleeping with someone else."

The more I explained, the more his face seemed to display his anger.

I went on, "This other person was a girl named Jasmine; I KNOW you're aware of her."

I pulled out my phone and scrolled to the pictures of him and Jasmine I had took of them at the hotel.

He grabbed my phone and asked, "Where did you get these? Were you stalking me that night?"

"No…No…I wasn't stalking you. I--"

"DID YOU SHOW THESE TO NINA?" He asked.

I now see that showing these to him may not have been such a good idea.

"No, I didn't show her!" I said.

He sat back in his chair and said, "Kristina, sometimes what you see isn't what is actually there and sometimes what is actually there isn't what you see."

He handed me back my phone and asked, "Do you know who Jasmine is to me?"

"I'm not so sure now that you asked."

He then said, "Kristina, Jasmine is an intern here at the office; nothing more, nothing less."

He smiled and pointed at my phone, "Those pictures existence were made possible because Jasmine had someone attack her; some guy named Mike she was seeing. He attacked her because "allegedly" she threatened to release some none flattering photos of him participating in gay activities. He assaulted her and she fled the scene. In all the chaos, she dropped her wallet and didn't have her ID. She knew I didn't stay too far, so she called me to help her check in to that hotel; she was scared and was looking for protection. I stressed to her the need to contact the police if she feared for her safety; but she very firmly insisted that we don't.

My mouth dropped, I could not believe that I was so far off track on the truth train.

"I'm so very sorry, Darin; I did not know. Oh my God, I feel terrible!"
I began deleting the pictures from my phone.

"Jasmine has called my house and Nina said she seen Antonio leaving work with her. Do you know anything about Jasmine seeing my husband?" I asked.

"I'm sorry, I don't know anything about that," he said.

"That's fine; I'm just embarrassed by how wrong I was about you."

He smiled and said, "It's okay, you saw what wasn't actually there. Now, let me show you what was really there that you actually missed."
I leaned forward anticipating what he was about to reveal to me next.

He said, "The reason Nina really wanted a divorce is because she wants to have a child and I can't have one.

108

She wants a family more than anything in the world. When I finally told her I'd agree to adopt a child, she didn't want to anymore."

I started to think about my family and how Nina has made herself right at home….in my home.

He continued, "She'd love another big house, nice car…..two little girls, maybe."

I slammed my balled up fist against his desk.

"THAT B***H!" I said loudly.

Thank God his office was so far back from everyone else's. I have to warn Toni about what she's up to.

I got up from my seat and Darin followed suit. I reached out for a handshake; he pulled me closer for a hug.

"I hope everything works out for you and Antonio; I really do," he said.

"I hope you find happiness, Darin."

We let go of each other and said our goodbyes.

Before I made it down the hallway, he stopped me,

"Listen, I'm not a divorce attorney. But I am good friends with one. Just in case you need one, here's his card. Also, take this package he and his office put together. It explains everything you need to have prepared, in case of a divorce: bank statement records, any type of evidence you may need to present in court, blah blah blah. You may find it handy."

I took the package of papers, "Thank you so much, Darin. Hopefully after Toni and I have a peaceful conversation tonight, I won't need these. I will definitely go over them and take heed to the information inside for future notes."

"Wonderful; be blessed, Kristina"

"You're going to be okay?" I asked.

109

He laughed and said, "Don't worry about me; I think I'll be able to manage."

I left Darin's office with just as many questions as I originally arrived with - new questions. I knew Toni wasn't home from work yet, so I texted the only person I felt okay speaking with, Calvin. I told him I didn't want to meet at his house, but instead at an old picnic area by the lake where we use to visit years ago.

I make it there first and await his appearance. He arrives and had a troubling look on his face. He seemed to have been heavily intoxicated; his shirt collar was stretched and pulled opposite of his neck.

"Calvin, are you okay?" I asked.

With his words slightly slurred he said, "I'm fine, I'm fine; what's going on with you?"

"I think Nina is purposefully trying to come between me and Antonio."

Calvin began to look away out into the lake. He seemed a little uninterested or unconcerned with my marital issues at this point in our rekindled friendship.

"I'm sorry if I'm boring you with all of this," I said.

He turned to me and said, "Oh God, no. I'm sorry, my mind is elsewhere this afternoon; I have a lot going on mentally."

"I can totally understand," I said.

We both looked out into the water; watching some nearby ducks walk along the lakes edge.

He then asked, "So you're sure she's the sole person trying to come between you two?

"Well yes, I believe so," I said. "Why'd you ask that?"

"Oh, just thinking of all angles she could be coming at you. You don't think Toni could possibly want a separation as well? He asked.

"I did, but now I realize it's her manipulating a** that's behind all this."

"Explain to me what all you've gathered to lead you to this conclusion," he said.

I go over everything I've noticed and I've felt. I even told him what Darin had told me just hours earlier. After I went over all the details, I explained to him that I was going to be confronting Toni about the entire situation before I went to speak with Nina. For some reason, Calvin didn't seem to like the idea of me speaking with Toni about it. He said he was afraid that Toni might lash out at me. Maybe Calvin felt that way because I mentioned to him how Toni choked me before. Calvin wasn't too pleased with that either. But regardless, Toni and I have to have this talk.

"So tonight is the night," Calvin said.

"Yes, as soon as he gets off work tonight."

"Alright, well good luck, Kay. I love you, girl."

"Thanks for being there, Cal."

We get up from the bench; hug each other tight and part ways.

Once home, I give the girls a call - they really cheer my spirits up. Their little voices can turn my frown to a smile in a matter of minutes. I hang up with them and go to the kitchen to get myself a shot.

After a few shots, I began to think about how Nina has literally been trying to take my husband from me. I get up from the couch I was on and went to the guest room where Nina was sleeping. I was anticipating

111

the pleasure of packing her stuff up to throw it out the door. But I open the door and realize her things are gone. I'm surprised, but that's good, the b***h better be gone; her time here has ran its course.

I felt excited that Toni and I finally had the house to OUR family again. She must have sensed the tension and decided to move on her own. Whatever it was, I was relieved; I almost wanted to celebrate. I just needed my significant other to hurry home.

***

Night falls and Toni stumbles into the house, his tie untied and draped around his neck. The look on his face was one I had never seen before. He sat next to me on the couch, his elbows on his knees and his eyes gazing into his interlocked fingers.

I asked him what was wrong, he said, "She's dead."

I jumped up and asked, "Who's dead??!" He looked up at me and said, "It's my fault, I let her die. I knew something wasn't right and I continued with the procedure anyway," he explained.

Being that he's a doctor, he should be use to things like this; this time was different though. I grabbed his hand and held it tight. I began rubbing his back; he seemed very depressed. I started to wonder why he was so stressed about this particular woman. I understand that a death is tragic, but my husband's reaction to the situation was almost as if I had died.

I asked, "Did you know her?"

He looked up at me and said, "No, I didn't know her at all. But her boyfriend was there and he--"

He stopped mid-sentence and turned his head towards the counter where we had our alcohol bottles. He got up and was about to make himself a drink. At this point, I was starting to get upset with his slow responses. Maybe it was just me wondering about my husband and this woman that has him all shook up.

As he reaches for the bottle I yell, "Mr. Antonio Kinsey, are you going to finish answering my question? *And he*, what?" I asked.

He grabbed the bottle and filled his cup up.

He then said, "It's Dr. and no I'm not going to answer your question right now Krissy. I'm really not in the mood to talk about this anymore. I'm home, I'm fine and the kids are okay."

He took a swallow of his liquor and paused.

He looked around and said, "Where are the kids?"

I smiled and said, "Well tonight...I was thinking...maybe we can have a little time alone. We've been through so much lately. My emotions have been running wild and I know you've been working hard, so I sent the kids to your Uncles house today," I said, while grabbing both sides of his tie, which was still draped around his neck.

He put his cup down and walked off.

Disappointed with his reaction I pleaded, "Aww c'mon Toni. It's been forever since we...you know."

He headed up the stairs and said, "Come to bed, Krissy."

I yelled out, "For what?! You won't even f**king touch me!"

He stopped in his tracks, turned around, and asked, "What did you say?"

Oddly enough, I was nervous, mad, and turned on by the anger I saw in his eyes.

I replied, "You heard me."

He stepped back down the few stairs he had traveled, walked directly up to me and grabbed me by the neck. He then held my head up with one hand. As I was about to open my mouth again, he slapped me in the face! That's when he pulled my face closer to him. We started intensely kissing and lip biting. He pulled off the flimsy dress I was wearing. Our hands began to explore each other, right there at the bottom of the staircase. In only my panties, he turned me around and made me lean against the wall next to the bookshelf. I heard his belt rattle and his pants drop to the floor. I felt his heavy hands travel across my body, making an indentation at every turn. *SLAP!* He slapped my bottom and I jumped a bit. He pulled my panties down, almost ripping them off and then...he put all of him inside of me. Oh my God, I don't think I can ever get use to his size. After many years of marriage, you would think I am by now.

As he continued to thrust and pull my hair, the books from the shelf fell to the ground. Making a mess, I thought, "Well there's more clean-up work for me." But that was just a brief thought while we changed positions. He began to go faster and harder and then pleasure turned into just pain. Then he removed himself *from me* and released himself *on me*. He stumbled back and wiped the sweat from his face with his sleeve.

Halfway out of breath he said, "You happy now, Krissy."

I pulled my panties up as he stomped his way up the stairs. I went to the downstairs restroom to clean up. I look at myself in the mirror and said, *Oh Kristina, Kristina, what are you doing? When are you going to tell him?*

I wash my hands and proceed to the other room where we made our mess. I started to pick the fallen books off the tile. Ah, my favorite read, "*Last Words to a Dying Heart*" by Dr. Linq.

Then the sudden feeling of deja vu sets itself upon me. I could have sworn I've picked up these exact same books before.

I remember it so clear now! The day I came home from Cakes, Cookies & Coffee, these same books were on the ground in the same fashion. I remember the drops of water I saw leading from the stairs to Nina's room. Then BAM! It hit me…Toni and Nina were f**king in my damn house, just like we finished doing!!

I run upstairs to our bedroom; I immediately jump in Toni's face.

"You f**ked Nina in my house?! I'm my house Toni - with my kids here sleep?!"

He held my hands back and said, "I think you should really calm down, Krissy."

The tears began pouring from my eyes, "I knew it man,

I f**king knew it! How could you do me like that, I did everything you asked of me Toni!"

"Oh my God, I can't believe you!"

I slid against the wall onto the floor and put my face in my lap.

Sitting there trying to stop my tears, Toni says, "Are you calm now, Kay?" I lift my head up and he drops a manila envelope onto the bed.

I sniffle and wipe my tears with both my hands.

"What the hell is that?" I ask.

He sat down in the bedroom lounge chair; he then pulled out a cigar and started searching for his lighter.

"Why don't you just open it up, Kay?" Very calm was his tone as he began to light up his cigar.

115

"Don't smoke in the house, Toni!"

As I was holding the manila envelope, I started telling him what I had been eager to tell him this entire time, "Listen Toni, Nina has been poisoning your mind! Her marriage is over and she's looking to replace Darin with you! She wants our family and you fell right into her trap!"

"Open the damn envelope, Kristina Jackson!" He yelled.

I paused; he hadn't called me by my maiden name since we've been married. I grabbed the envelope and opened it up in front of him.

The tears just began flowing from my eyes. I couldn't believe what I was looking at!

He watched my reaction as I looked at what was inside and then he said, "I don't think "*Nina*" is the one trying to break us up Kristina...it's you."

I stood there looking at photos of me and Calvin! Photos from when we had coffee together. There were photos of us laughing and hugging. Then I saw photos of us having sex on his couch! I fan through the pictures in complete disbelief.

"Where did you get these?" I asked.

He sat there still puffing his cigar with a non-emotional stare on his face.

"Does it really matter at this point, Kay?"

"Stop calling me that!"

He laughed and said, "There's nothing more to say; I'm sorry Ms. Jackson."

I pleaded, "Toni...baby look, I know…...I know these pictures are wrong….I'm wrong…but baby--"

I tried to talk but the knot in my stomach was so tight; the lump in my throat was so large it limited my speech. I couldn't do anything but cry! I walked over to where Toni was at; I just wanted to touch him.

"Oh my God, I'm sorry....It was Nina....She set all this up! She was trying to break us up from the beginning!

His eyes focus on the bedroom door entrance and he stands up; Nina walks in draped in an all red dress, a pair of red heels and matching red lipstick.

"Toni, are you done with her yet, baby?" She asked.

I yelled, "B***h have you lost your muthaf**king mind??"

I push off Toni and immediately ran over to Nina. I couldn't wait to get my hands on her! I was literally about to kill her. No this b***h did NOT just call my f**king husband, *Baby*. Before I could reach her, Toni grabbed me and pulled me back.

"Let me go!!" I screamed.

He stood in between us and said, "Hold on little lady, just hold on."

"I'm not holding on s**t, she's the reason we're dysfunctional now!" I said.

With a smile on her face she said, "I'm not the one who was f**king another man on a raggedy couch."

"Toni, I swear to God if you don't get this b***h out of my muthaf**king house right now, I'm killing you and her! GET OUT OF MY F**KING HOUSE!"

Nina laughed and said, "Oh my God Toni, would you please tell her already."

I looked up at Toni and he had this stale expression on his face.

He slowly began to back away; he looked down at me and said, "Nina isn't going anywhere, Kris."

"Not going anywhere?" I asked. "What in the hell do you mean?"

He didn't answer.

I said, "Antonio Kinsey--"

Nina cut me off and said, "Dr. Antonio Kinsey."

"Shut the f**k up!" I said.

"ANTONIO, what is that supposed to mean?" I asked.

Then he said, "I want a divorce, Kristina."

Shaking my head in disbelief I said, "Wait, what? No, no...no...I've made mistakes, you've made mistakes, this can be fixed...we can fix this! SHE'S THE PROBLEM!"

He cracked a smile and said, "No Kris, I'm your problem. I wanted a divorce the entire time. We've lost the chemistry we once shared; the love we once had. I knew the only way to make this divorce end in my favor was to make sure I had proof of your infidelity."

He looked at the photos scattered all over the bed and said, "I think I have everything I need now. The funny thing about these photos is, you gave me the private investigators number, Kristina. It was the day you accidentally brought Nina's book home. When that happened, I knew it was meant to be. Nina just made sure my plan worked out perfectly."

He started laughing and said, "Coincidentally, I think Nina and I have become a little closer than expected. You know the only one who was surprised at that surprise party was you. *Surprise!* Oh...and don't worry about the kids, they'll be well taken care of; being that you're not as...*well off*. You can visit them sometimes though...maybe."

He then picked up a picture off the bed of Skylar in her *Fuzzy The Bear* shirt - her legs with small bruises on them.

He continued, "I wonder how Sky got these marks on her little legs; I hope mommy didn't do it. It would suck if I tried to give you visitation rights and later find out that you are harming the kids."

Betrayed by the one person I thought I could go to hell and back with – I couldn't be anymore hurt.

I looked at him and said, "You're a f**king coward!"

"I prefer *Jerk* but to each his own," he replied.

"I'll f**king kill you if you try to take my babies away from me, **I promise you!**"

"I think you should leave now, Kristina."

Then out of nowhere all three of us are startled, "*No one is going anywhere!*"

Calvin stumbles into the bedroom pointing a gun directly at Toni. He was clearly drunk, even worse than earlier. It seemed as though he'd been crying; his eyes were blood shot red.

Nina jumps back from Toni and says, "Calvin, what do you think you're doing?!"

Toni starts clapping his hands, puts on a big smile and says, "Calvin, Calvin, Calvin; you're just in time for the show."

I was not only shocked to see Calvin here, but also scared of his intentions.

I quietly ask, "Calvin, what are you doing here?"

Toni then said, "Hey Cal, why don't you put that gun down and tell your f**k buddy over here how you work for us."

Toni then reached on his top dresser drawer, grabbed an envelope, and tossed it to Calvin.

I look over at Calvin and asked, "What is he talking about? What's going on?"

Toni started laughing and said, "Whoa-ho-ho, this should be interesting!"

"Shut your f**king mouth," Calvin said.
He now aimed the gun at his face; Toni raised his hands higher and continued to smile. Nina stayed in the corner with very little to say.

Toni continued, "You think it was a coincidence that he just so happened to be at Furniture City and Cakes, Cookies & Coffee at the same time you were there?"

Calvin took a deep breath, looked over at me and said, "I don't work for him. Him and this b***h over here asked me to sleep with a woman and allow them to have photos taken of us, unknowing to the woman. I needed the money; business isn't as well as I would like. But when he asked me, I didn't know it was you! Until that day I saw you at the party. I wanted to say no, but $5,000 I couldn't resist. I figured I'd eventually tell you…but then it's like I started to fall back in love with you all over again. I didn't know *how* to tell you...I'm so sorry, Kay."
He lowered the gun as tears began to fill his eyes.

I simply replied, "You son of a b****h."

Toni laughed some more and said, "Love is in the air now isn't it!? You got your money; I paid you. Now put your gun away and leave!"

Calvin raised his gun back up and said, "Oh…I'm not here for the money."

Toni looked at him confused, "Well what the hell are you here for?" He asked.
Calvin displayed a menacing expression on his face. He then asked, "June 10, 2014; Does Regina Price ring a

bell?"

Toni's smile completely disappeared.

Calvin screamed, "YOU TOOK HER FROM ME! That baby... That baby inside her was mine! You lied your way out of it before…I will not let that happen again! Toni held his hands up high and pleaded, "Yes, yes, I remember. But look Calvin…in the Medical field…accidents happen, my man! I mean….hey I'm not the only one in the hospital working, bruh! You can't blame me, blame the team!"

I noticed Calvin's finger sliding closer to the trigger.

Gun gripped firm in his hand he said, "You think I was working at that hospital by accident, you piece of s**t? When you told me you would pay me for this stupid little game you wanted to play, I figured I'd use some of your money as my going away cash after I take you out! You should be in jail and without your license - or dead!"

I intervened, "Listen to me Calvin; you don't want to do this! Think about the life ahead of you. Karma will take care of him; put the gun down."

"Just put the gun down, Calvin!" Nina pleaded from across the room."

"TELL THE TRUTH!" Calvin demanded.

Toni dropped to his knees and begged Calvin, "OKAY, okay, it was my mistake! She died because of me. I decided to wait for the emergency operation. At first we lost the baby, then the mother followed. I'm sorry…. LOOK, I'LL LEAVE THE CITY! YOU WANT KRISTINA, HAVE HER! Just let me live; I have kids!"

"You're right, you really are a jerk," I said.

"I'm not going to kill you," Calvin said as he pulled out a tape recorder. "I think I have everything I need now."

Toni dropped his head in relief, but when he looked back up, I think he knew his life would never be the same.

Then Calvin glanced over at me and said, "Let's go Kay; you don't have to leave with me, but you're leaving this house tonight. I can't allow you to stay here with this a**hole anymore."

I grab the pictures off the bed then my purse off the nightstand and followed Calvin out the room. As I was walking out, Nina runs over to Toni to console him while on his knees still. I turn around, ball my fist up as tight as I can and with all the power in my body, I land a punch right in the middle of her face! She screamed and grabbed her nose as she fell flat out on the floor – I then kicked her in the stomach.

"Dirty b***h!" I said as I exited the room.
I make it downstairs and out the house.

Just before Calvin got in his car, he turned to me and said, "So what now?"

"I don't know; I guess it's time for Kristina Jackson to find herself," I said.

He replied, "Yeah, I can understand that. Aye, I want to apologize for everything. I just--"

I interrupted, "No need for all that, you don't owe me anything; I owe myself. My faults are my faults."

"Understood," he said.

We got in our cars and rolled our windows down.

So where you headed now?" He asked.

I smiled and said, "To go get my girls."
We drive off and head in different directions.

As I travel down this dark road on my way to get my babies, I can't help but cry; but also a feeling of relief

122

comes over me. I know I should feel like I lost something, but sadly enough I feel as though I gained so much more.

Lesson Number 16: *"It's hard to lose someone you realize you never really knew."* Everyday people we do not know pass away and we don't even shed a tear. Why, because often we don't feel a connection to people we've never seen, heard, or touched. But what happens when that same outsider lives with you; touches you and holds you? What happens when that person tells you they love you? What happens when you realize you're actually *in love with a stranger?*

Epilogue

Three months later Toni and I finally had our final day in court; the divorce is official! I ended up using the attorney Darin recommended and he turned out to be a great choice. We decided to sell the house and split the money 50/50; I kept my car and he kept his. We both were awarded joint custody; I was excited that my babies would still be with me. Toni is ordered to pay alimony until I get some steady income. I didn't even want his money at first, but my attorney insisted. I sold the pink diamond ring he gave me – I didn't need to see it anymore. It was a reminder of a time I didn't want to revisit.

I ended up getting a new house on the other side of town. It's not as upscale as I'm use to, but it's peaceful, and that's all I can ask for right now. I still keep in contact with my old neighbors. I actually gave Stacy a personal apology; I sent her a cheesecake with the words, *"I'm sorry"* on it.

I started back party planning again and my first test subject is Skylar's 4th birthday; I'm thinking of going with a Disney theme. Hopefully I can get that business off the ground again; I have plenty of time to focus on it now.

Calvin and I still keep in contact and he's still trying to *make things right* between us…whatever that means. I just need some single time to myself. I need to know what *Kristina* wants out of life; I think I've lost track of that. Some things are better left in the past anyway.

I haven't seen Nina since that night at our old house…and I think that's best. My old neighbor Michelle told me she still works at Mercy Medical. I'm sure it's going to be real boring up there without Toni on the job. Calvin and Regina's family took their little tape recorder to a lawyer; the lawyer decided to take their case. In the coming weeks, Darin will be representing Calvin and The Price family in their malpractice lawsuit. The odd thing was that on the night Calvin confronted Antonio about the death of Regina, Mercy Medical encountered another loss during a normal pregnancy.

One thing I've learned, communication is truly the key. Never be afraid to at least talk to your significant other about how you're feeling – maybe you can solve a problem before it becomes one. Even though Toni and I are now divorced, he's still the father of my children. I may have a bitter taste in my mouth about *how* the situation took place, but I'm in a good space now and when you're good, you have no reason to wish harm.

Lesson Number 17: *"If you have to **fight** for your marriage you have to ask yourself, who are you actually **fighting**? More than likely you're **fighting** against the person you believe you're **fighting** for...and in that, it's almost impossible to come out a winner."*

.......or is it?